Alone Against the Sea

A boy struggles with his impending manhood through tragedy, understanding, and love, as he faces his future.

Set in the early 1990s, with a few alterations of Caribbean geography.

To Ari

May you have a steady hand at the helm of your life's journey.

ISBN: 978-1-7370065-2-7

More about the author, his blog, and discussion forum can be found at:
https://www.lancepacker.com

Alone Against the Sea

Lance V. Packer

MJV

Contents

Preface

A few words may be in order first. I make no claim to be a sailor with a lifetime of experience voyaging the world's seas, nor extensively sailing a specific portion of those seas. In keeping with my inclination over the years, to dabble in all sorts of experiences that catch my fancy, my sailing experience is varied.

I must admit, though, that my interest in the sea goes back to my early youth, when some of the first memories I have of reading were about boats, the sea, and sailing—from single-handed round-the-world voyages in the early 1900s, to submarines in WWII, to mid-century undersea explorations of pioneers such as Cousteau. It all sounded exciting and interested me greatly.

So, I was primed to set out on my sea adventuring at an early age. Yet, being from a farming background, it wasn't until I was on my own that I was in a position to get myself on the water. My first boat was a wooden 23' outboard cabin cruiser, which I converted into a commercial salmon troller. This brought an interesting and sometimes challenging window into that particular lifestyle in Southeast Alaska.

Next was a 30' sloop, a little stock sailboat which got my wife, son, and me into some great cruising territory, including that of humpback whales, who breached alongside us, and glaciers which dumped ice floes to bump our hull during the night, while anchored. There are many tales from those times.

Our next boat was a 49' center cockpit sloop, which we bought with the intention of sailing during our summers off from teaching in Alaska. Although we put in a sabbatical winter season in the Bahamas, we soon realized that this was not a practical plan; we still had too many years before retirement, our son was getting older and had new interests, and the boat was too big for us. We sold it, to go boatless for a few years more.

Retirement came at last, and so did *Different Drummer*, our next boat, this time a 39' catamaran. I had been interested in trimarans and catamarans from my high school and college days onward. The concept of more than one hull was fascinating, so I thought it was time to investigate, as is my custom.

We spent six months during the winters for four years exploring the Bahamas, and moving farther south each year— off-shore for days at a time, as well as island-hopping—to the Turks and Caicos, Dominican Republic, Puerto Rico, the U.S. and British Virgin Islands, and Saint Martin. After that, it was time to turn around and sail back—in a few months, downwind—to Florida, where we sold the boat.

Now, I am back in the Caribbean with another 39' catamaran, *Mariposa*, for more small adventures and an escape from cold, wet winters. I just need a warm abode which I can move from island to island, learn about their living inhabitants—human and non-human—and visit the wonderful world of life beneath my floating home at will, while dreaming up tales such as the one you are about to read.

PART ONE

1

The black of the starless Atlantic night formed an impenetrable backdrop to the undulating watery stage of waves and foam as a small sailboat performed its rushing dance toward an unseen destination, hundreds of miles beyond. It rose, twisted, and faltered with the swelled sea, then fell again, into the rhythm of the wind and tumbling waves.

Light from the mast running lights cast a slight glow upon the taut, white sails, but even this disappeared into the gloom of the night, a few feet from the boat. In the open cockpit, a movement, a seeming phantom, riding this steed into the unknown; a sailor was plying his calling.

Gregory shivered slightly and pulled his jacket tighter about himself, not so much against the cold—for in this tropical air it is rarely actually cold—but more against the blackness, which seemed to send fingers of inquiry into every loose fold of his being, and seek a toehold of doubt for the incubation of that greater challenge, fear.

No matter how many night passages he had sailed, night watch was always unsettling. There were some, he had to admit, which were not so bad, such as when the stars burned brilliantly overhead, or when the moon was sufficiently full to almost radiate a warmth of its own.

No, those nights weren't so bad and almost enjoyable. Yet, there always lurks the possibility of the unseen, and that was why he insisted on watches being stood, either by himself or his son, now sleeping below. Even out in these desolate spaces of the ocean there are dangers, primarily from a collision with small, poorly-lit inter-island freighters, or semi-submerged shipping containers lost during a distant storm, or even yachts deluded into the habit of running unlit because of the false security of the vastness of the sea.

The sea doesn't care, Gregory thought, *only humans do, if they are of a mind to.* He shivered again. These thoughts, so easily brought on late at night, seemed to only get worse. He deliberately shifted focus and stared blankly at the red glow of the compass centered before him.

Gregory was not a large man, but was built for endurance. His middle-age years were still fairly well hidden in the slightly boyish face, emphasized by a broad grin which crinkled the corners of his eyes. He was normally clean-shaven, but for the last few days he had let this ritual slip, and now had an irregular shadow of discoloration about his chin, making his tiredness even more pronounced in the darkness.

Yes, the night—in fact, these last days of sailing—was taking its toll, and he felt the need for rest.

Time to change watch, he decided, and David's sleeping form below slowly coalesced in his mind. His face cracked slightly in a smile of relief.

His son. Yes, David could relieve him from the aches which now stiffened his body. The thought of the sandy-haired, thin-faced boy sleeping below, probably dreaming the sweet dreams of youth at this very minute, filled Gregory with pleasure.

And David was indeed deep into the depths of teenage fantasy. He rustled fitfully on his bunk, as his mind's eye carried him deeper into his dream…

He's struggling to find something, ill-defined and uncertain. Colored shapes around him move in and out of his vision, his grasp. Hard, rocky ground presses against his hands and feet uncomfortably. What he's looking for is supposed to be near him—warm and comforting; feminine.

Yes, it's the girl who has appeared in his dreams before, laughing as she dashes from rock to rock, behind one dense forest shrub then another. He can never get her to stop and hold still. But if she did stop, would he call out to her? Doubtful. His courage with girls has always been fleeting, so why would it be different now?

And there she is again, just standing quietly, as if waiting for something. What? Waiting for what? Could it be for him she's waiting—for him to say something? Time is slowing down, moving as dense as syrup.

David tries to call to her, but his mouth will barely open, and the only sound he can force out is a sort of groaning, "Wuh-h-h-h!" Yet, his mind is alert. He knows he's failing, but his body will not do as commanded. He tries to call again and again. The girl starts to slowly turn, as if to leave, and he strains harder to call out. But something is pulling him back, restraining his every attempt to turn to her, to call out…

"David! David!" Rough hands shook his shoulder.

He moaned lightly, "Wh-u-ut! Wai-ai-t!" More shoving at his body, and he suddenly pushed back at the thing tormenting him. "What?" he growled, half-awake, then looked up.

His father was standing above him, outlined dimly in the light, his thick, brown hair windblown and the yellow foul-weather jacket shiny, as trickles of sea spray found their way to the cabin floor.

"I need a break for a few minutes. It's going to be a long night, and I need you to stand watch for a while." Gregory looked more closely at his son, gave him a light shake to get an answering nod, then turned back into the main cabin of the boat. Leaning heavily to one side, to counter the angle of the heeling boat, he lurched at the companionway stairs to gain access to the cockpit again.

David groaned, foggily. *Yuk!* He hated to go out and stand watch at night while they were under sail. Especially on nights like this, when it was pitch-black outside—no moon, just a few stars poking indiscriminately through the darker inkiness of the clouds.

You can't tell where the water ends and the sky begins. You can't even see the bow of the boat, for God's sake. Ugh! He rolled over in his bunk, tighter against the port side where he was downhill, so to speak, and tightly wedged into his bed.

Gregory waited for his son, but he never came. *Still, the trip down below did me some good,* he thought. He was more awake now.

He stared at the glow of the compass rose. It rolled and tilted, but always swung back to their heading: 127^0 southeast. A thin grin spread on his shadowed face, as he thought of the trusty little autopilot humming down below in the engine compartment, unfailingly steering them toward their destination.

He glanced outside the dodger which only partially covered the sloop's open cockpit, but quite effectively broke the main force of the spray, and the 17-knot wind which blew steadily just aft of the beam, slightly downwind.

A good wind for making progress.

In four days they should be off Puerto Rico, then into the Virgin Islands. At least after that they could take it easy for a while, instead of pushing on as hard as they'd been doing.

Gregory thought of his son, obviously having fallen back to sleep—seventeen years old now and trying to grow into his rangy, almost-man body, which was already nearly as tall as Gregory. Growing into a man's mindset of responsibility was another matter, however.

David seemed immature, given to excessive daydreaming and flights of fancy—at least Gregory thought so—and this was a challenge he constantly struggled with. Now David was probably asleep and dreaming again.

The thought sat soggily in Gregory's mind for a few minutes, and he slowly drifted back to thinking about the task of sailing. He glanced at his watch: 11:15 p.m. *Well into night now. The sails look okay; on course.* Another look around: nothing to be seen.

I guess I can make it a while longer, he thought. *Maybe another half hour until it's his full turn at watch. Not much sense waking him for only a few minutes of rest just now,* he reasoned.

He settled back comfortably against the cabin, under the protecting dodger. The rushing, gurgling water swept by and lulled him into the rhythmic, lifting roll of the sea swells. And the small boat was swallowed into the blackness of the night, its white stern light dipping behind the swells, growing dimmer, dimmer, and eventually disappearing.

2

The murky dream shapes were moving about David once again, but this time more boisterously, swaying and rolling with an unfamiliar rhythm which sometimes seemed to lift him free of the hard, rocky ground and toss him frantically into the air, clawing and clutching at whatever might be near, to save him from a certain tumble. But nothing was near.

David rolled up against the chain locker door at the head of his bunk and, as he groggily awoke, he felt his body lift quickly with the bow of the boat, then be dropped airborne. His head hit the small locker door; the sharp pain jolted him further awake. *Damn! That hurt!* He quickly rolled upwards on his bed, against the heeling of the boat, just in time to save himself from another resounding crack.

The heavy thud of water against the hull and following hissing sound forced him to take further notice of his situation. *Heavy seas or the wind has changed,* he numbly thought. The bow lifted again and bit into the oncoming wave, but this time the boat didn't shudder as before, and seemed to work more comfortably.

He lay there sprawled out, hands grasping the edge of the bunk, his mind still half-caught in the dream. The murky shapes were still slowly swirling in and out of his thoughts, but had mostly settled into an impenetrable haze which refused to clear. David reconciled himself to the fading dream, and gradually forced his awareness into the present.

He stared at the darkness of his cabin. The boat was sailing smoothly again, though somewhere above a sail was flapping noisily, demanding attention. *Wind must be changing,* he vaguely thought. *Dad should be adjusting the sails.* But the beating continued.

He pulled himself into a sitting position and ran his hands through his tousled hair. Then, pulling them down to his face, he rubbed his thin fingers over his eyes, to hopefully clear his faint vision in the small cabin. Braced against a bulkhead wall, he groped around on a shelf for his watch.

Finding it, he pressed the light button and held the watch close to his face, to read the digital numbers: 4:30 a.m. An involuntary groan rumbled in his chest, and he lay back down again to drift in and out of sleep, in hopes that the dream would return.

After several lengthy, fitful attempts for it to reappear, he finally woke up enough to conclude it wasn't coming back. He sat up silently, rocked by the rhythm of the boat, before he sighed in resignation and shoved himself off the bunk. He was sort of hungry, anyway. *Might as well get up and see what Dad's doing.* He stumbled toward the galley and companionway.

Stopping to grab a couple of cookies, he climbed barefoot up the companionway ladder for a couple of steps and peered up into the cockpit. The steering pedestal, with its compass binnacle light casting a slightly reddish edge of highlight to the cockpit shapes, dominated the center. The metal steering wheel glinted coldly as it moved in short, little jerks, in response to the commands of the autopilot. The blackness above was filled with the sounds of the sea swirling past, the humming of the wind through the rigging, and the snapping of the luffing sail. Everything seemed in place, except for the sail.

So, where's Dad?

A blanket piled with some cushions, against the cabin under the dodger, showed where he must have curled up for comfort and some sleep, but that was all. The sea and wind chorused loudly, and the boat rhythmically slid off the crest of one unseen swell, down to meet another. David stood there, not yet quite fully awake, but enough to be dimly aware that something might not be right. *I'll check it out.*

"Dad?" he cautiously called out into the open cockpit. His voice still had the slight croak of male adolescence but was approaching the huskiness of manhood.

"Hey, Dad!" This time he called more forcefully and deeply. No response. *He's out on deck,* he finally concluded, as he climbed up into the cockpit and looked forward, over the protection of the dodger canvas. The force of the wind and a misting of spray immediately snapped him fully awake. It was pitch black out; nothing could be seen ahead or at the side.

"Dad!" This time his voice was stronger, more strained from the necessity of fighting the pressing wind, but also from a rising panic within. His voice lost in the void, he called again and again, still no response. Pulling back into the protection of the dodger, David slumped down heavily on the cockpit seat, and tried to force his perceptions into some kind of logical sense.

If he's not up here, he's got to be… down below! Dad must be below somewhere, of course. He grasped at the idea and tumbled down the companionway ladder.

But where could he be? His mind raced. *It's such a small boat, but where else…?*

He groped and found a cabin light. There was the galley to starboard, on the left was the port navigation table and electrical panel, forward was the small dinette, and opposite a settee seat. To starboard were the head and toilet, and forward of that was his cabin. He lurched to the head and jerked open the door, where he flicked on the light. The gleaming white toilet stool greeted him with a wide grin.

As he reached to snap off the light, a reflected image in the mirror above the sink grabbed his attention. His longish shock of hair was disheveled and his white T-shirt was twisted awry— but what disturbed him most were his eyes, wild and fearful in their green depths. He had always worked hard at faking being cool and collected, especially when trying to impress girls or friends. *But, what's that face? Who's that frightened rabbit?*

Dad's cabin! the thought exploded. *Of course, he's there!* And David tumbled the short distance back to the nav station. His father's berth was just aft of the chart table, under the cockpit above. David reached and hesitated. *But, what if he's…?*

He pushed aside the folding door to the small enclosure and numbly stood there. The small ship rose and fell with the waves, unmindful of the dawning terror within its protective hull.

David reached forward into the dark and felt the pile of covers on the bed. He knelt on top and stretched farther back, to mindlessly finish the task of searching the rumpled bedding.

No one there.

What the hell…? This doesn't make sense.

The swelling storm of fear that had been gathering burst upon him.

Dad's gone! The thought and words boomed in his racing mind. *He's gone! But… where?*

His throat swelled tighter, choking the rising well of emotion which struggled for release. "Hey, Dad!" he called out. Then again, more forcefully, "Dad?" Finally, it erupted: "Dad!" he screamed, in more childhood terror than he had ever before felt. Tears flooded his eyes, smearing his vision as he screamed again, and clawed his way to the cockpit once more.

But there was no relief here, either; his blurred gaze revealed the same scene that had greeted him before. Crying and shouting into the wind, David turned his attention to the inky, wet deck forward. Knowing somewhere within himself that this effort was also futile, he nonetheless lifted himself out and around the dodger, into the wind and spray, to stumble along the cabin sides.

He held tightly to the grab rails and mast stays as he made his way forward, his vision clearing somewhat in the coolness of the air. Finally, he was near the bow. The quick rising and falling of the boat at that point made him stop. He could see there was no sense in continuing; there was nothing beyond.

The spray off the bow was heavy and he was getting soaked. The mainsail fluttered and snapped above him—the source of his first awakening. He looked up briefly and caught a glimpse of a few pinpricks of starlight, piercing the clouds which swiftly scudded by. Glancing down, he stepped up onto the cabin top, clasping his arms tight to the mast, and looked out beyond the perimeter of the boat.

The sea was not to be seen, only felt. Felt not only by the motion transmitted through this small ship, but felt also as a presence, something which you knew was there, vast and important, but not seen. It was a chilling sensation for David, cold and alien; terrifying to him now.

He stood there clinging for some time. His tears had stopped and his throat was not so tight, though still raw from crying out. Wetness and chill forced him to finally move aft, back to the protection of the cockpit, where he sat down heavily under the dodger and gathered the blanket around himself. He again gave in to uncontrolled sobs.

The steering wheel continued its little dance of jerks and turns, and the mainsail still snapped in the wind, protesting its lack of trim. *It just doesn't make sense.* He slowly regained control of his crying. There was no logic to it all. *How can he not be aboard?*

Through clearing eyes, David stared numbly at the cockpit's shape and contents, unconsciously going over each little detail. At last, his eyes stopped at the steel railing at the stern, just aft of the steering seat, behind which the water swirled and gurgled, as it smoothly led out from behind the boat. Something was different, though he couldn't quite place it. Soon, his awareness cleared and focused.

Yes! That's it: it's gone! The horse-shoe life-ring is gone!

Excitement rising, he scrambled back to the railing. And the man-overboard pole, too! *They're both gone!* His mind leapt to gather the implications of this discovery. His dad was in the practice of trailing a knotted rope with a float astern, which was tied to the ring and pole; "So if anyone falls overboard, they can just grab the rope, and the gear will be pulled out to aid in their rescue."

Well, if it's gone then he fell overboard, David's thoughts raced, *and he's at least got a chance with those to hold onto!* But the sudden welling of hope was dashed, as he looked out at the total blackness astern, and felt the wildness of the sea and wind. He could see absolutely nothing, and a sense of overwhelming desperation returned.

But I have to do something! he thought, as he struggled to reclaim his confidence. *Maybe Dad's only been gone a few minutes. Maybe he's back there waving at me, waiting for me to come back. I've got to go back!*

David thought of the time. *How long? How long have I been up now?* He felt his wrist for the nonexistent watch. Quickly, he looked into the cabin, at the chronometer on the bulkhead: 5:00 a.m. *God! A half-hour. Has it been that long since I first woke up? What've I been doing, for Christ's sake?* He remembered drifting in and out of sleep.

Grimacing with anger, he turned to the cockpit to take action. Then, he froze. Exactly what was he going to do? He couldn't see anything. The boat was on autopilot; the wind would be in the wrong direction; the sails were up... and... and... so what could he do?

Well, shut off the damn autopilot! He reached down to the control panel. Immediately, the boat began to round up into the wind and waves. The sails luffed with cracking gunshot sounds, and the controlling sheets snapped like whips in the air. The boat rolled and pitched tremendously before David finally reached to turn on the autopilot again, and it steered the boat back onto its previous course. Recovering from the panic of that experiment, he contemplated the next option.

He could lower the sails and start the motor, then he could

go back against the wind—not easily, but supposedly it could at least be done. The motor was no problem; he had started and operated it many times, while anchoring and powering from place to place. He felt heartened by that thought.

Then there were the sails… and his growing optimism plummeted. That was different; it was sort of a mystery to him. Oh, he understood the theory and all—where the lines went, and so on. Well, sort of, he had to admit. He had never shared his dad's enthusiasm about sailing and more or less envisioned himself as a passenger on his father's dream.

Not that the effort to teach had not been made—he had been enrolled in a sailing school class, and his dad always tried to teach him more while on their boat—he had just never been a willing student. Consequently, he never truly learned what he had been exposed to. Now David cursed that student. *Why didn't I pay attention?* Sure, he would help out on *Endeavor* if his dad asked, but the fear of being able to control all the power in those white, billowing tower clouds had petrified him, and he never got over it—never cared to. And now the fear held him prisoner.

He stared at the taut lines wrapped around the winches and felt the vibrating strength of the sails transmitted through the mast and hull. It brought the boat alive, and he was an unwilling rider on this tightly-reined beast.

Tears rimmed his eyes again and his throat tightened. His frustration rose as he cursed the thing within him that had made him so obstinate, refusing to take an interest and learn what was now so vital.

He cursed the impossibility of his situation and despaired at the realization that he had to do something. It was his dad out there, his father, the man who took care of him and bought him cotton candy and took him on carnival rides and… David's mind slipped back momentarily to memories long forgotten—to memories of his dad and him as a child.

But he had to do something, and quickly! Blackness leapt at

him from all sides. Even if he was able to get the sails down and the boat turned around, then what? Where would he look? His dad could have disappeared hours ago.

In frustration, his thoughts rambled over the problem and possibilities, and a vague remembrance of earlier that night wriggled its way to the surface.

Dad tried to wake me earlier. What was it he wanted? His mind struggled to remember and finally did: *He wanted me to stand watch while he caught some sleep.*

And, with that last memory, David sank yet even lower into depression. "My god, *I* did it! I killed him," he sputtered. And, tears streaming, he threw himself back against the cockpit side, horrified by what he had remembered.

3

David huddled against the cabin bulkhead, his throat aching and tears blinding his vision. He pulled even tighter into himself and cursed his stupidity, his obstinacy, his arrogance, his... his... very existence. He walled himself off from the clutching awareness of the crisis, by wallowing in self-reprisal and pity, and he soon started to feel sorry for himself.

Why did Dad drag me off on this trip, after all? I didn't ask to go. I was perfectly happy back at home, with all my friends. Who wants to go out where there's nothing to do but stare at miles and miles of water, anyway?

He cleared his eyes with the back of his hand, and his chest loosened as he began cursing the boat, wind, sea, sails, monotonous food eaten, work he'd had to do, places they visited... And, as memories of places they had visited rolled into awareness, his cursing gradually ceased.

Other memories, recent memories, also floated in on the tide of anger. *Well, some of it was okay,* he let the admission slide in. His mind rambled for a moment, then stopped as he remembered the time his father was trying on hats in the Nassau Straw Market in the Bahamas. His dad was determined to buy one—"I'll need it for the sun,"—but the choices were rather out of character for him. He and David broke up with laughter after he put on one particular hat with a very large brim and a fake bird's nest perched on top. The gaudy colors and size were completely out of character, but his dad bought it just on impulse. That was what was so neat about the moment: his dad never bought anything on impulse, let alone something as absurd as this bird hat!

And that was the image which halted David's orgy of pity, freeing him to swim back to the edge of this black pit of desperation.

"I've got to try to find him, damn it," he announced aloud, in a determined voice, and pushed himself up. His mind cleared as he stood, struggling to decide what to do first, and in a moment he carefully started to act.

Once again he switched off the autopilot and, as the boat rounded into the wind, he freed the sheets from the winches, so that the sails luffed freely in the wind.

With the boat now facing more into the waves, it was hard to keep his balance—yet, except for some violent lurches into a cockpit seat, he managed fairly well. The mainsail and jib immediately began flogging frantically in the wind, but the pressure was now off, so they began to slide down the mast and the forestay toward the deck as he let go of the supporting halyard lines.

Good, David thought, as he scrambled toward the sails. With one hand clasping the mast and the other clawing at the flapping expanse of the main, he gradually managed to get the sail to the boom and tie a couple of sail-ties around it. *Not very neat, but under control,* he congratulated himself.

Now the jib. Since this smaller sail was hanked onto the forestay, he needed to go all the way forward, to the very point of the bow, and pull the sail down the stout cable that reached the top of the mast. It normally slid freely to a nice pile in the bow but, now whipping in the wind, the upper half rode up and down the forestay with each pitch of the waves, like a jockey riding a racehorse.

David cautiously stepped forward on the tossing deck, as the boat headed into the wind. He had almost made it to the jib when the deck seemed to fall out from under him, and just as quickly rise, to momentarily toss him into the air. When his feet again made solid contact, he was three feet away from where he had left.

The deck slanted steeply as the boat rose to meet another large swell, and David instantly lost his footing and fell, sliding down the deck toward the railing, as a sheet of seawater poured over the bow. Slipping in the wetness, he grasped for whatever he could find, his mind blank with surprise. Before he could locate a handhold, the boat found him; he smashed against a leeward safety-line stanchion and into the safety netting his father had rigged, for such a need as David had now found.

Frightened and soaking wet, he lay for a brief moment in the security of the net, hands now tightly clamped to the supporting stanchion. His mind was numb with the swiftness of the event, and its seriousness. Slowly, though, another thought swirled about and finally took shape.

Was this what happened to Dad? Safety harness—I didn't remember to put one on. Maybe Dad didn't, either. The image of his father on deck, not wearing a harness, being tossed off the bow and missing the net, played through David's mind like a child with a video remote control. Again and again the scenes of possibilities ran, sometimes slow, sometimes fast: variations from the bow, walking along the deck, even being tossed out of the cockpit.

No, the cockpit scenario wasn't likely, he had to admit. It was most probably similar to his experience: in a moment of carelessness, Dad not heeding his own preaching about the use of a harness. With this image fixed in memory, it stripped away a bit more of the unreality of his father's disappearance.

Convinced of his conclusion, David carefully pulled himself along the deck to the cabin top and, grasping the grab rails, worked his way back to the cockpit. What a relief to get into that secure place!

But, now what? The jib flapped raucously and David tried to think. Something else was needed, but what? The violent tossing of the boat, now rolling sideways, finally made him realize what it was.

Control, we need control! With no sails, no control. So, start the engine, stupid! Cripes, how dumb can you get? he admonished himself, as he marveled at the simplicity of the decision. Scrambling to the steering position behind the wheel, he reached to the control panel and turned the key, then pushed the starter button.

The diesel immediately jumped to life with a comforting rumble, and idled easily, waiting for a command. David was never before so glad to hear that low-throated, rattling sound! A rush of warmth flowed to his face and he immediately felt better.

Pushing the shift lever forward, the vibration of the turning propeller imparted a new presence to the boat, one which David desperately needed. Gaining confidence, he nudged the throttle farther forward, and the boat began to respond. Turning the wheel, he gradually worked the bow of the boat more into the wind and accelerated, the jib still flapping away, but he didn't care—he was doing something.

The boat was now headed back in the direction they had come from. For a few minutes, David powered into the darkness, peering intently for anything that might show a sign of his dad. He had no clear idea of how that might occur, but for now just looking was enough.

Yet, the satisfaction didn't last long. Questions soon began to crowd in upon his newly acquired confidence, snapping at the hamstrings of his self-assurance, to bring it down for a quick kill. His mind scampered rapidly through the underbrush of doubt.

Exactly which direction am I supposed to look, anyway? Had he noted the compass heading? He quickly glanced down: 82^0. But what had been the heading before he turned the boat? If his father was back there, which way was "back there"? Another stupid act. And what did he hope to see? *It's pitch black out there!* He'd never see a man floating in a yellow horseshoe buoy in that darkness. He cursed his eagerness in looking.

Then he remembered the man-overboard pole. Did it have an automatic light? At the top, on the float, somehow it seemed that there had been, but he had never really looked at it. Deeper dejection and thoughts of stupidity followed. It seemed to David that he would never cease dredging faults from the quagmire of his character, and he briefly sank into the bog of self-pity again.

However, something had changed around him, and David gradually stirred from his malaise and looked around. He noticed that it wasn't quite as dark as before; it was getting lighter. *Daylight, it's getting daylight!* Soon the sun would be up, and his mind raced with the possibilities.

With this bit of encouragement, David set to searching the receding darkness, steering first in one direction for a while, and then another, vaguely consoling himself that he was somehow covering a large area of the sea where his father might be, patiently waiting in the vastness for David to rescue him.

The new day finally arrived as he searched on, and the wind slowly decreased.

4

From the perspective of a soaring frigate bird, the brilliant blue expanse of the sea seemed to extend forever that morning. Somehow supporting an inverted sky-bowl of unworldly purity, the now windless sea appeared smooth at first glance, but closer attention would reveal an undulating surface, a pattern set in motion as easterly swells spread from the direction of Africa. Finally reaching this far western edge of the Atlantic, seeking a beach or jagged shore upon which to release their wind-created energy, they then crash with a resounding whump and a hiss of foam. Long troughs and massive swells roll endlessly onward in ceaseless rhythm, lifting and lowering any object which might be floating on the surface of the broad expanse of seeming nothingness—such as the dot of a boat now bobbing listlessly upon the scintillating blue depths.

The small boat rolled with the swells, dropped down the troughs, and slewed about unguided at the top of the crest. Then down again, to disappear, reappear, and on and on, in ceaseless rhythm. A piece of flotsam drifting lifelessly, it would seem.

It was mid-morning now and David had been slouching on a cockpit seat for the past hour, trying not to think of anything, but just watching the swells roll by. But that was difficult; the image of his father, out in the sea, alone and waiting, continually interrupted his attempts. As the wind had dropped, the sun's heat increased, with only a few puffy clouds to now scantily dress the glassy cover of sky above. David had stripped to shorts and a cut-off shirt, but it was still too warm behind the cockpit dodger.

Finally, he could no longer put off what had been a morning ritual for his dad: rolling up the large plastic window so that fresh, cooling air could pour through and push out the dead air which would otherwise hang behind the dodger cover. But it didn't help much. The boat wasn't moving, just rising up and down; they needed forward motion, and then the breeze would come. But that meant a decision, and David wasn't at that point yet.

He had motored through the early hours of the morning, aimlessly looking and steering in all directions. He scanned the horizon, where each far-off waving pair of arms turning into a feeding seagull, each little speck on the surface playing evil tricks of deception upon his willing imagination. With every one of these, David grew more and more despondent.

At last, the absurdity of his search sank in. He had a while back shut off the motor and finally captured the flailing jib. He then plopped into the cockpit and was now still sitting there. *What do I do?* The enormity of all the factors and implications reduced his mind and body to jelly. He could do nothing. He didn't even know where to begin.

But his stomach did; he was hungry. With a faint glint of spirit, he raised himself and swung down the companionway, into the galley. Out of habit, he peered into the refrigerator. Apples, bread, lunchmeat, leftovers from last night's dinner, the meatloaf his dad prepared for tonight, a salad ready to eat... his father seemed to be everywhere. David grabbed a bag of bread, and settled on a peanut butter sandwich and an apple.

Back in the cockpit, munching his snack, he slowly began to feel some of the pieces coming together. First of all, what did he need to just survive? To him this mainly meant food. *I should be okay on that account,* he reasoned, since he was fairly well acquainted with the eating department. *Alright, what next? Water.*

He quickly got up, slid to the nav station, and checked the

water tank gauge: half full—that meant about 35 gallons left. *Not bad.* He reassumed his position in the cockpit.

Now what? His dad, of course. And with that, the unrelenting quandary and accompanying welling tears slid in again. *What should I do? What can I do?* He knew that time was foremost in importance if he was to find his dad, but how to do it?

Maybe it was already too late, or maybe it was just simply beyond his ability. The former possibility was quickly dismissed, since his dad had the survival gear, such as it was, and maybe a plane would spot him. But the latter was depressing and probably quite true. His throat tightened again in that cramped feeling, as if he could never breathe again, while he fought the tears back.

He had to admit that he couldn't even get all the sails down last night, let alone search systematically, and the thought hounded him. *And, where am I? I don't even know that, so how can I search where Dad might be?*

"What a friggin' mess," he growled aloud. The sound of his voice almost made David jump, so unexpected it was, but it was also good to hear something other than the constant sounds of the sea, and he felt encouraged by the break.

"Quit kicking yourself and get going. Do something!" he loudly admonished himself, in a voice which reminded him of his father's tone when David had been particularly obnoxious. *Alright, I'll do something! Give me a minute. Jeez!* He gave his habitual response and settled back into the cushions.

But that didn't last long. Nothing productive resulted from his pout and, besides, he was getting tired of the inactivity. *Anything will be better than doing nothing, even if wrong!*

The logic of that thought forced his mind to focus more determinedly. *Like what? What can I do? Start searching again? How and where?* The image of his father floating out in that watery expanse, growing weaker—but fervently hoping and expecting his son to find him and pull him to safety—was too much to bear. David once again shook with waves of guilt. *I can't do it, even if I want to. It's just beyond me.* The hellish images tore at his body and mind.

Yet, after what seemed to be ages, another image gradually rose its head, tentatively at first, then equally as clear. *What would Dad do? What does he want me to do?* The idea arose that maybe his dad was floating out there as calmly as possible, trying to conserve energy, and would realize the extreme difficulty for his son in being able to handle the boat, let alone find him in the darkness and vastness of the sea. Despite these problems, he would be hoping for level-headedness in his son.

No, Dad would want me to do something logical... like get some help. Get help! He'd hang on. That's what he would do... and expects me to do.

And so the battle of images and emotions continued.

5

As the boat bobbed along with the passing swells, while David's mind and body fought with each other, the rhythm of the boat's movement, and watching the measured passing waves, gradually had a calming effect on him. He began thinking again, and didn't let his emotions continue their rampant control of his being.

Although a brooding cloud of guilt at his inability to search for his father clung to his thoughts, David finally made a decision: his experience with the immensity of the sea thus far had decisively convinced him that he needed to continue onward, to someplace where he could get help, taking his dad's advice.

But he certainly wasn't able to do anything if he didn't know where he was. And besides, he had enough problems just trying to operate the boat. With that much decided, no matter how unsatisfactory, he reluctantly went back down below, to the nav station, to attack the "Where am I?" problem.

David glanced over the layout of that small corner. Outside of the small chart table and seat there wasn't a whole lot to look at. His father wasn't one to "…clutter up my mind and sink my pocketbook with a bunch of gadgets." David could remember him saying just that, when the two of them were in a marine store buying items for the trip.

David had been looking at the electronics equipment and was especially taken with the radar screens, radio-beacon receivers, LORAN-C consoles, etc.; their intricacies of buttons and digital readouts fascinated him. He didn't know how all of these things were able to help a person with navigation, but they sure looked interesting.

He could just imagine himself sitting down below on the boat, twiddling dials and pushing buttons—that seemed like something worthwhile doing; meanwhile, his dad could do the steering. But instead, that day they just bought an inexpensive VHF radio and one of the new GPS units just coming available, and left the rest sitting on the shelf.

And there the radio now lay in a corner. David stared at the small, black instrument, dead to the world, just when he thought he could use it like his dad had wanted: for emergencies. It was broken. David had seen to that.

Well, it wasn't really his fault, he tried to console himself, but he knew better. He had dropped it.

No, face it, I threw the damn thing at the chart table, when it couldn't cut through the static while I was saying goodbye to Darlene, he reprimanded himself.

She was the one he had met off a boat in Georgetown, before they set south from the Bahamas. She was kind of special, and he especially wanted to say goodbye one last time before they left the next morning, but the radio was cluttered with static. *So, was that a good reason to throw it? Now look where it got me!*

His dad just muttered, "Damn," when he came to see what the noise was, then turned away. David was relieved at the moment that he didn't get chewed out, but the silence ended up hurting a lot deeper.

Remembering this made all his previous childish outbursts of anger pour back out of the garbage can of humiliating moments, like an infestation of maggots, and he had to struggle hard to get the lid back on. *Childish!* He wasn't going to let it happen again… he hoped.

Next to the radio were several gauges and a switch panel for the electrical circuits. Above that, on a shelf, were numerous books. Some were cruising guides, which David had glanced at previously, and he knew others had to do with navigation, because he noticed his father consulting them when he was using the GPS and calculating their position on the charts.

Gregory liked the idea of doing navigation the old way— paper charts and position fixes—but using GPS instead of a sextant. It was an expensive device, yet he figured it added a lot of safety.

He picked up the GPS unit, not much bigger than a transistor radio, and carefully looked at it. He pushed the power button. In a few moments, it blinked in block letters, "SATELLITE RECEPTION LOST. REACQUIRE."

Now, what the hell does that mean? He tried hard to remember the several times his dad had tried to explain the GPS to him, but could only conjure up his lack of attention and his dad's frustration. *More stupidity!* His face flushing in shame, he struggled to visualize what his dad did with the GPS.

Well, it was something to do with charts. Which made sense, he thought. *I guess that's as good a place to start as any.* He lifted the hinged tabletop to dig around.

Finding one which looked familiar, he pulled it out and placed it on the table. It was a small-scale chart covering many miles and islands, designed for passage-making. There were Florida and the Bahamas, Cuba, Haiti, the Dominican Republic, Puerto Rico, and finally the Virgin Islands, their destination. But that encompassed a thousand miles, just in a straight line between points. *Too much water!* So, he began to examine the chart more closely for their recent landfalls.

He knew they had just left the Bahamas—or were going to be. They had recently stopped at several small islands, to do some skin-diving and beachcombing. He knew Conception Island was one, and Rum Cay another—he thought those were the names. It seemed like there were a couple of really little islands, too, but what their names were he didn't know. They all sort of ran together in his mind, after a while.

So, how do I sort it out? As he scanned the chart and dug through the nav desk for different charts of a larger scale, his thoughts drifted back to last winter, when the idea of the trip was first brought up...

6

His dad and Rachel were in the living room talking, when he came home from a friend's house. He said, "Hi," and walked on by to his room. He noticed that his dad's charts were spread out on the coffee table, as they often were, but paid no special attention. After raiding the fridge, he cheerfully plopped into a chair and commenced eating a sandwich. No one said anything for a moment, then Rachel spoke up.

"Your dad and I have something to talk about, about this spring and next summer." She paused and added, "It's not anything you're in trouble about." It wasn't necessary to put that in, she immediately realized, but she was so used to being in a reprimanding role that it just slipped out.

Although it had been seven years since she and Gregory were married, she never did feel that David accepted or even barely tolerated her. "I think you two will have a great time." She tried to smile warmly.

David stopped chewing and looked from her to his dad.

"Your mother…"

David wished he wouldn't use that word; *She isn't my mother,*

"…is trying to say that I've got an idea I think you'll like, after you think about it. So, give it a chance and hear me out, okay?"

David looked at his father, his slight frame leaning forward, elbows on both knees and hands clasped—tensed but controlled, as always. *So, get on with it. What's the big deal?* "Okay, so?" David replied casually, and recommenced eating.

With a mixture of relief and warming enthusiasm, Gregory

leaned back against the couch, hung a leg on a knee, and put an arm around Rachel, pulling her slightly against him. "We think it's about time you had a little change in your life here— something to break the monotony of 'the same old thing'," Gregory mocked David's perennial complaint.

David made a quick face and ate on.

"Besides that," Gregory removed his arm and leaned forward again, "I need a change, and I think you and I need some time together. We're all busy around here, you with school and stuff, Rachel with her job, and me with mine. We all pretty much do our own thing and actually don't spend much time together."

He paused to see how it was registering on David's face. He felt Rachel's hand press lightly against his shoulder. "So, I figure the only way to be able to have time together is to get away from here, since we don't seem to be able to find time as things are. Get away somewhere, out of the routine, take some time off. How does that sound?"

"Fine, I guess." His sandwich finished, David started peeling an orange. Having stretched his act of indifference about to the limit, he added, "So?"

Irritated, Gregory went on, as Rachel squeezed his hand a little tighter. "Now that we've got the boat berthed down in Florida, it's in a good spot for taking off to the Caribbean, down through the Bahamas to the Virgin Islands, at least. After we get there, we'll see what we want to do."

While letting the effect of his words sink in, Gregory reached out to paw through the charts for a moment, then pulled one out to spread, his slender fingers lightly smoothing the creases where it was folded.

He wasn't tall—more muscular and compact than anything— but his features were almost delicate, like a woman's. Despite this, he enjoyed outdoor work and physical labor, though his job in the architectural office limited the opportunity. His love of sailing provided a welcome outlet for change.

"So, what are you saying? We're going to sail to… the Virgin Islands? Who's we, and exactly when is this supposed to happen?" David slid his eyes to land on Rachel.

Rachel's firm grip on Gregory's tensing shoulder stopped him from replying. "David," she started, "I can't get away from my job very easily for any length of time, so I can't go. Besides, I feel this should be a time just for you and your father to be alone. You need to spend some time alone, without me," she added. Raising her fingertips to brush back some of her coal-black hair, she gathered herself. "I'm in the way sometimes, between you two…"

"Now, let's not get into—"

"No," she interrupted Gregory, "let me go on." She turned back to David. "I just want you to know that I get how you feel and that it's okay, I don't hold it against you… you should know that by now, but I just want to make it clear. I realize I'm the latecomer in this family, and that things can't ever be like they were with your mother, but it doesn't mean they still can't be good. We can still have a fine family life; it'll just be a different family, that's all. I think that's something we all have to accept, not just you, David."

She watched him finish peeling the orange, then make his blank *"And…?"* expression.

"So, I'll hold down the fort here while you two go have a good time." She smiled to lighten it. "I've got friends at work to do things with, and I've got a million projects around here that I can never finish up, because of you two lugs always being in the way." She gave Gregory a pull toward her and laughed lightly. "I'll be just fine here. Don't worry about me."

David glanced up from splitting the orange, stared at her, and popped a section into his mouth.

"As to when," Gregory picked it up, "I figured you could miss the last month of school by getting your studies done early, or take some with you if necessary, and leave Florida by the second week of May." He concluded, "How does that sound?"

David hesitated. "Okay, I guess," he drawled, and tore off another section of orange. Inside, though, he was struggling with a rising tide of anger.

Feigning cheerful acceptance of his son's reply at face value, Gregory went on to outline his plan.

Later on that spring, David still wasn't enthused about the idea of spending the whole summer alone with his dad, especially on that dumb boat. He truly didn't have any big summer plans, he just didn't want to miss out on anything that might happen with his friends, and be left out of all the catching up next fall, when they gathered in the first few days of school to fondly remember the escapades of summer.

When he casually mentioned the planned trip at school one day, some of the gang agreed that it was a really dumb way to spend one's summer. But others thought it would be kind of neat—at least it would be a change of scenery and something different to do, instead of the usual boring routine. However, none of this was any help in making him feel better about the trip.

By the end of April, he finally finished up his class work for the rest of the school year and they left, with David still obedient, but dragging his heels.

And now here I am, staring at this stupid chart. He blankly looked at it, then started to scan more carefully.

But, wait a minute!

His eyes fixed on a thin pencil line, drawn in with his father's unmistakable draftsman's precision. Alongside the line were

letters and numbers and little circles, drawn carefully every so
often. It started at Florida, continued to Nassau, on down past
the Exumas, and on to... then the line stopped. Or rather the
side notations did; a lighter line continued onward to a group of
islands.

David looked closer: Turks and Caicos Islands. *So, that's where
we were headed next.* He vaguely remembered the name in
conversation once, but hadn't attached any significance to it; to
David, it was just another name among the many. Just another
piece of rock jutting from the sea. He looked back along the line.

This must be the last entry Dad made. A small circle around a dot
on the line had the note *"23:30 hrs"* written next to it. Eleven-
thirty at night—that was the last time he noted their position on
the line. The image of his father sitting at the table late at night
loomed before David, and the terrible distress grasped at him.

It was probably just before... Hounding memories of the startling
realization last night again pressed upon him, and he pivoted
away quickly from the thought, forcing himself to concentrate
on the task at hand.

Okay, he tightly gathered his thoughts, *so, we were to go to the
Turks and Caicos. Well, I can still do that, since they're the closest.* All he
had to do, he told himself with feigned assurance, was to
continue along his dad's dead-reckoning line, and he'd get there.
Simple...

But, how? the ugly question raised its head, but was quickly
shoved away. *I'll just start the damn motor and steer it there,* he grinned.
Marvelous!

He immediately clambered up the ladder and started the
engine. The penetrating vibration and husky sound were
welcome companions. He started to shift the gear lever when he
suddenly realized he didn't know which way to go.

Stupid! He reprimanded himself, and scuttled back down
below, leaving the engine on. He looked at the dead-reckoning
line and found what he needed: 127 degrees southeast.

Scrambling behind the wheel again, he pushed the gear lever forward and the boat began to respond. More throttle, a turn to the compass heading, and he was on his way.

The boat rolled badly without the stability afforded by the sails, and the loose lines slapped noisily against the mast, in loud, ringing blows with each lurch. The sails, poorly lashed down, slid back and forth with the movement. David noticed these things but tried to ignore them; it was only temporary, anyway. When he got into a port, he'd take care of them.

But, after a short while he began to tire of steering; it was a constant battle to keep the boat on course with the rolling action. It finally occurred to him to turn the autopilot back on and, after some experimenting at getting the right course, he was relieved of this task. *This is okay,* he thought, and settled down to a mid-morning snack in the cockpit.

After an hour of travel, however, he suddenly arose, startled from his stupor, and hurried below. Reaching the nav station, he flipped on a switch labeled *"Fuel"* and watched the needle: one-quarter full; maybe ten gallons. He'd never make it; it was too far. He groaned aloud in despair, once again foiled in his logic.

Numbed, he slowly climbed the ladder, paused, then angrily pulled back the throttle and gearshift lever. He shut off the motor and autopilot, and sat fuming as the boat slowly came to a standstill.

Tears rimmed his eyes, and he felt like he was choking. A rage was boiling inside, and at last it exploded. "Damn! Damn you!" he yelled at his father. "I never wanted to come, anyway! Why did you bring me here?" His last words were drowned in uncontrollable sobs, as his shoulders heaved. "Oh, shit!" he wailed, and hung his head between his arms, crossed on top of the steering wheel.

He gave in to utter frustration. His last reasonable chance of escape had been taken away—escape from this horrible nightmare that never seemed to end, but kept dredging up new obstacles, one after the other. The rage stormed on as he fell to the cockpit seat and cried.

But the empty ocean never answered his desperate wailing. The listless swells rolled the boat back and forth, and it clanged and groaned in protest. Nothing paid any attention to him, and time passed, wave by wave by wave.

Now he ached. His throat was sore from the strain, his eyes felt like sandpaper, and he had a headache. And it was getting hotter. He pulled himself under the shade of the dodger and stared blankly out at the water. Images rolled through his mind—images of past fits of anger and the ensuing results.

Well, getting mad sure won't do me any good here, dummy. Oh, it got him something whenever he was visiting his mom; he'd get some results, despite her intentions not to let him have his way. But even then, later on he always felt bad about it, never good. And now he felt bad again, having blamed his dad for what had happened.

Christ! David cursed himself. *He's out there somewhere trying to stay alive, and I'm blaming him!* Now David was mad at himself, and his face glowered angrily. But that was no good, either; he was only feeling sorry for himself again—another childish game to play.

Shaking his head in an attempt to clear the mess cluttering it, he stood and looked around. Nothing to be seen. No help in sight. Nothing. He was all alone… and he had to face up to it.

7

The sun was high overhead now, and gave the sea a color of blue, which was at the same time sparkling clear, yet impenetrably deep in hue. David leaned over the side of the boat and idly thought of being immersed in that blueness, with nothing but thousands of feet until the bottom—getting darker and darker, until pitch blackness consumed everything.

With his fantasizing mind tumbling down in gut-wrenching freefall, he suddenly broke loose, and in fear jerked back into the safety of the cockpit, thankful that he at least had this boat to put distance between him and the depths.

Jarred back into awareness of his problem, he protectively half-stood up and looked quickly all about him, into the distance, over the bow, the sides, and aft. Nothing but miles upon miles of water. And, somewhere out in it, his father. David shuddered as he imagined his father out in those depths, without the boat to also give him needed distance.

As a kid, he was afraid of the water, and it took several years before he enjoyed the water at all—in a pool, that is. After that, it took some getting used to, swimming in the lakes located nearby. They were busy places, with their early morning mirrored surfaces quickly shattered by speeding ski boats, windsurfers, paddleboats, fishermen trying their amateurish hands, and fleets of sailing dinghies from the recreation center. Then there were the beaches, of course, with hundreds of splashing kids and young people, bothering the old folks who just liked to sit and float in their plastic air-chairs. At any rate, the water was well used, and any monsters which formerly stalked its depths had long since escaped—but it took a while for David to be convinced of their absence.

Having his friends swim below and jerk his feet off of the firm beach bottom never helped matters. And, when he was older, the same friends then attacked while he was swimming to the diving raft, and down he'd go. Only when he started attacking others did he begin to vanquish that particular fear.

When he was twelve, his dad enrolled him for five days in a dinghy sailing school. He wasn't too keen on that venture; boats were always tipsy to him, and sailboats especially so. But the young college guys and gals, with nice tans and youthful enthusiasm, did a spirited job of teaching. He managed to get around pretty well after some rather scary moments, and he found he could control the small boat well enough by the last day.

He remembered his dad standing on the shore, shouting encouragement when he was having a tough time making the boat go anywhere, then cheering loudly when he returned from a long tack out onto the lake and back. He was embarrassed by all the fuss but, at the same time, he didn't tell his dad to stop it, either.

Ah, yes, Mom was there, too. She cheered for him and clapped exuberantly. But the show didn't last long; the family never went anywhere without some kind of argument taking place—not for as long as he could remember. Whenever David was out of the limelight, and it was just the two of them again—Mom and Dad—this icy wall rose between them, and never melted until he was present again. But he could feel its coldness, even with their efforts to hide it. The chill eventually tainted everything he had to do with his parents, regardless of which one it was. So, he just started wrapping an insulating layer of isolation around himself—and when that felt good, he'd add yet another layer.

Now here he was, out in this great big lake in an oversized dinghy, with nobody standing on the shore to cheer him on and offer advice. But there also was no icy wall to worry about, either. And the relief of that observation pushed his feelings of depression a little farther back into their cave.

Slowly, the realization that there were some benefits to being alone—away from all the past—filtered into his awareness and solidified into some welcome feelings of confidence, as his thoughts turned to focus on the rocking boat beneath him.

It heaved and fell with the waves, creaking and slapping with its boat sounds, becoming less and less a lake-bound dinghy. It emerged newborn in his mind for what it indeed was: a small ship in need of a master, someone to give it direction and free it from the weakness which now bound it. It needed care and devotion—even love—if they were both to survive unscathed on the sea.

David reached out to the steel wheel and felt its slow movement, in response to the tugging waves on the rudder. He laid a hand on the sun-warmed teak cap rail which ran along the hull-deck joint, from stem to stern, and tenderly stroked the solidness of the golden wood, as if absorbing strength from that ancient building material.

His eyes swept to the mast, strong and stalwart, rising in defiance to common sense, like a long middle finger giving someone the bird. He smiled at the thought, and also felt pride in having such a symbol on his boat.

A symbol of what? Defiance, he finally concluded—defiance at the impossibility of such a thing as a sailboat being feasible. *What a ridiculous thing!*

David grew warm to the idea; this pile of wood and fiberglass, metal and cloth being able to float and get somewhere, against the forces of the wind, sea, and people. An impossible task! But here he was, out on one of those preposterous human imaginings, which was just drifting around, waiting to go somewhere. And, with that thought and growing confidence, he determinedly swung below to the chart table.

"Let's get this baby moving," he muttered and pulled the chart to him, as he sat and leaned forward on his elbows. *First, I need to know where we are. Now, what was it Dad did?* He struggled to remember. A vision of his father working at the chart table and showing David what he was doing began to materialize in David's mind—not clearly, but enough to serve as a touchstone to other images and instruction.

He had to assume some point of reference, someplace to begin. That would mean a GPS position. *Yeah, that's what Dad did: he used the GPS to get a reading…* But here it got harder to remember. Some numbers on the little screen his dad would read and mark on the chart… *Right!* Now he could see his dad doing that… *But what numbers?*

David looked closely at the chart. There were some numbers his dad had written on the dead reckoning line he had drawn: 23°05'25.7"N 74°12'41.5"W.

So, that's where we were when Dad also wrote in the time. The spot was next to the *"23:30 hrs"* entry from last night. *And where are we now? Well, what did Dad do?* Again, stretching his visual memory, he watched his dad take the GPS unit out into the cockpit, push a button, look at it, go down to the nav station, then do something with the chart.

David took the GPS up into the cockpit, pushed the ON button, and stared at the screen. After five seconds it activated, and small lines began to fill out into solid bars. Shortly, it stopped. Then, he noticed down in the right-hand corner new numbers. *Yes! That must be where I am now.* He raced down to the chart table and settled in. *Fine, then I'll just plot my progress like Dad.*

He stared carefully at his father's neat line. *Now what?* His eyes wandered around the nav area. He looked up at the bookshelf suddenly, scanning the titles until he came to one with the title, *Navigation: Simply Explained.*

Well, that's something promising! He genuinely didn't like to read—especially old, dry classroom wallpaper, like textbooks on the bookshelves—but this might help out.

He looked at the D.R. line and, after mulling over some images of his dad working, and reading a brief section in the navigation booklet, he put a dot on the chart, drew a new line, circled the dot, and wrote in the time and location. "Looks about right to me," he concluded, with satisfaction.

With his navigation plan resolved, David smiled with pride at the new heading to the Turks and Caicos, and went up on deck to get ready for the next step. *Now we've got to get moving—and that means sailing.* And, as a help, the satisfaction of his final day's effort at dinghy school washed into his memory, and deposited some solid driftwood on David's barren beach of confidence.

He set about getting the sails ready to raise, working half out of memories from sailing school and visions of his dad on deck, and half out of logic, by following the lines where they lead, and what needed pulling where. When he was finally ready, he started the engine, put it in gear, turned the wheel to bring the boat heading into the now rising wind, and set the autopilot, to make sure the boat stayed that way.

Okay, now the sails. After moving forward to the mast—safety harness on, this time—David began pulling on the main halyard line, to hoist the mainsail to the top of the mast. By now, the sail was slating noisily as the twelve-knot breeze tugged at it, shaking it in rippling rolls, like the neighbor lady next door used to do, as she stood on the second-floor balcony shaking her oriental rugs.

Now, quick, the jib! He began hauling on the jib halyard. It went up smoothly and soon was also noisily slatting, shaking the mast rigging.

Suddenly, something cracked David solidly on the side of his head. He reeled back from one of the wildly whipping sheets tied to the end of the jib. The instant pain was intense and he swore loudly at the flogging lines, but he also knew that only he was to blame, and he had to get them under control fast. Throwing several loops around the winch, he pulled one jib sheet tight… and raised his hand to rub the spot where a large bump was forming.

While David was absorbed with these tasks, the boat had started to veer off from the wind, and the sails began to fill. He now quickly set the autopilot to steer farther away from the wind, to speed up the process, and the boat started to heel over, as the sails began to fill even more. In short order, the boat began moving forward, picking up speed rapidly.

It also started heeling too much and David almost panicked, until memories and images of the past again rescued him. Turning *Endeavor* into the wind, he dumped air from the sails and the boat slowed, becoming more upright. With the wind again filling the sails, more gradually this time, he reset the autopilot. No longer needed, he took the engine out of gear and shut it down.

The boat soon settled into its familiar rhythm of movement, and the chorus of humming rigging and creaking hull rose to enliven the air. As the boat gained speed, the old gurgling and swishing sound also joined the song. David gripped the wheel tightly and grinned broadly.

I'll be damned! I've got it going. I've got the old lady going. "Alright!" he laughed aloud. "I'll be a son-of-a-bitch! How about that, Dad?" he called out in exhilaration.

He took a glance around, in an unconscious search for the once-reassuring waving arms and shouts of encouragement, but it didn't matter that there was no response—he felt good about himself; a warm feeling that he was doing something that mattered, and doing a good job of it.

But it was more than just that. He also had the odd sensation that he could stand back, off the boat, and see himself there at the wheel—steering confidently, looking up at the sails, reaching over to tug at a sheet for trim, then leaning back to study the sea ahead. Only, it wasn't him at the wheel.

Or, rather, it was and it wasn't. It was a disturbing feeling, as though it were him and his father together… only there was just one person at the wheel.

8

David continued sailing all that day without any real problems. Once set, the boat fairly steered herself. Gregory had been attracted to that particular feature of *Endeavor* when he was searching for a sailboat. The 36-foot Taiwan-built boat was designed along the lines of a modified traditional full keel and strong seaworthy construction, but at the same time had more modern innovations of rigging, and interior accommodations which made life at sea substantially easier. Since Gregory had envisioned the vessel as a focus of family life, these factors were of importance.

Although the sloop-rigged boat had a fiberglass hull and cabin for easy maintenance, it also had teak exterior trim and interior cabinetry, which added that touch of warmth and class he had always admired in sailboats. Beauty doesn't help a boat sail better, but it does make the sailor proud. And Gregory was proud of *Endeavor*.

Of course, the autopilot was now a great help to David, but he tried to use it as little as possible, since it took electricity to operate and electricity meant running the engine, which brought him back to the fuel shortage problem. So, he resolved to use it only when truly necessary, such as when he had to do something on the bow, or go below to get something to eat or relieve himself.

He pulled down some more of his father's books on sailing and made some headway through them, but he soon grew tired of the diagrams and terminology, and set them aside. Besides, he seemed to be doing pretty well anyway.

Except that he hadn't been able to find his father. Everything was going great except for that one oppressive fact of reality. Even as he headed away from the location of his father's accident, he couldn't help unconsciously scanning around for something that would bring impossible hope. But it all looked the same—every direction, every wave, every cloud, and every bird soaring overhead or skimming at wingtip over the swells. The only provision for his mind's stability was the unvarying compass disk in the cockpit.

Eventually, like the lightly drifting fog which he had often watched with his dad, as it set in upon the evening stillness of backwater Chesapeake creeks, the hopelessness of any possible search by him was reaffirmed, and tainted David's newly gained confidence.

However, he was right. His dad was right. He couldn't do it alone. He needed help, and the nearest aid was in the direction they had originally been headed. There was no choice.

And, late that afternoon, the tiny speck that was *Endeavor* continued sailing onward upon the vast, blue expanse, heading toward the southeast.

That evening, as the sun started to set, David watched the orange-red colors spread across the horizon cloud bank, from north to south, then stretch high overhead, where they faded into a pink nothingness. Shortly, it began to get dark, and it suddenly occurred to David that he had another problem on his hands: how to keep going during the night.

He could, of course, simply take the sails down and drift, but then he would again be in the situation of not knowing where he was, until he read the GPS when he awoke in the morning. More importantly, he'd lose distance and time—especially if he made errors—and he needed to get to a port as soon as he could. No, he had to keep going on a direct, purposeful course. He'd have to rely on the autopilot only when absolutely necessary, and he murmured a soft thanks to his father for putting that little angel aboard.

With the sunset, darkness rapidly settled about him. The sensation he had was of shrinking smaller and smaller, until even the boat itself seemed to disappear in the blackness. But the boat sang with its creaks, groans, and wind vibrating the mast, and the waves swished and gurgled alongside the boat to keep him company. Soon his eyes became adapted to the dark, and he was able to find groups of stars which were periodically exposed by gaps in the clouds.

Even the sea itself seemed to be helping accustom him to the strangeness of his journey, since occasional minuscule flashes of light appeared at the crests of waves, as they gently collapsed in foam. These welcome scintillations were even more prevalent around the boat, winking away as the vessel created her disturbance in the water. The tiny plankton which emitted the light seemed to glow, in recognition of David and the boat's passage—sort of like passing through the ranks of the Roman legions on the night before a battle, as Caesar reviewed the troops, David reflected, as he let his mind ramble about a film he once saw while an impressionable child. And so, to the muted roar of a host of thousands, he rushed onward through the night, in his blue chariot pulled by two white stallions of sail.

At about one o'clock in the morning, David was finally worn out and falling asleep. He set the autopilot and curled up in a cockpit corner, leaning against the cabin bulkhead in a pile of cushions, covered with a blanket. He tugged at his safety harness line, to make sure it was securely snapped to a cleat, and immediately dropped off to sleep.

He was jostled awake at about four o'clock, when the boat responded to a shift in the wind. Making the necessary adjustment, he chided himself for sleeping so long and, after taking a look around, set his watch alarm for one hour later.

That next awakening was brief and, although there were unmistakable signs of dawn coming soon, he quickly fell asleep again.

David didn't awaken again until about six-thirty, when the sun finally reached above the cloud bank on the horizon, and its rays lightly touched his face and eyes. Stretching and yawning, he looked about, then quickly checked his watch. He was somewhat unhappy with his inability to stick to his awakening schedule, but the disappointment didn't last long; he had made it through the night, and the boat was still moving along on their new route— that was very satisfying.

He lay back to savor the moment and watch the day come alive, with the reddened sky gradually changing to a light blue, and the black sea birds gliding over the wave crests, wingtips lightly grazing the surface in search of prey. A few flying fish broke the surface just off the bow and skipped along the water, one by one smashing into the sea, as their momentum and the lifting air failed.

He stretched one more time, stood up, and set about the ship's daily business.

9

In the afternoon, David tried fishing. He and his dad had previously caught a few small jacks while sailing, but David always hoped for more—something like a big marlin, he kidded his dad, although he had no clear idea of how he would handle such a giant fish. Regardless, he once again clipped a likely-looking lure onto the line and reel they had mounted on the stern pulpit, and let the line out. Just barely able to see it darting back and forth under the surface, he sat down in the cockpit, to steer and wait.

He had almost forgotten about the line when he heard the reel whine, and turned to see something rolling and flashing in the sun. The line was taut and singing. Startled into action, he jumped up and started to reel. It wasn't a really big fish; when it was closer he could see it was another small jack. *Okay,* he casually thought, *you'll still make me a meal.* And he began to reel harder, since the fish was only several yards behind the boat.

Feeling the strong pull, the jack gave a sudden lunge for freedom, as it broke the surface and shook its head. Like a spring released, the line and lure sprang backward like a shot. At the instant the fish shook, David knew it wasn't good, but it all happened so fast that he couldn't move. There was a sharp sting and tug on his left shoulder, then, looking down, he saw the four-inch lure hanging there, with one of the hooks buried to the shank.

David just stood for a moment, staring at the clinging object. It didn't hurt much; in fact, he barely felt its presence, except for the slight pull of its weight. But it was there—disbelief or wishing wouldn't make it go away. He quickly flipped on the autopilot to take over the steering, and sat down. *Now what?*

He gingerly lifted the hook away from his shoulder. A small mound of flesh moved with it. *Oh, jeez, I've really got it in,* he realized. *I'll have to cut it out, but which way? Push it on through and cut off the hook, or try to back it out, cutting the flesh away from the barb?*

He decided pushing it through might be best; it looked deep. Then, biting hard on the heavy nylon line, he freed the lure and himself, and stood up to go below for his tools.

Instantly, his head reeled slightly, and he could feel the blood draining from his face. *Great,* he thought, *just what I need.* But there was little to be done; his body would have its way and go through the familiar reaction. He sat heavily onto the cockpit bench and lay back with his knees bent high. A slight ringing sound echoed about him, as swarms of white dots swirled before his closed eyes.

In a few moments, he felt better enough to do the job, and carefully lowered himself down below. He rummaged around somewhat blindly, since his light-headedness was returning, but he managed to come up with a blade. It was a replacement blade for one of Dad's tools—not the best, but it was clean and available, and at this point that was all he cared about.

Wedging himself on the settee to keep steady, David carefully pushed the hook, to make the point go on through and out. No luck; too much distance to go. *Okay, I'll back it out, then.* And he tugged. A little progress was made, so he resolved to follow that path. But, getting the hook to back out wasn't easy; the barb resisted every move, and with sharp bites of pain.

With a fish on, it took lots of care to keep the hook barb in. Now, when he didn't want it to catch, the barb hung on very well. *An unjust revenge,* he reflected with a grimace, as he tugged harder.

Inserting the tip of the blade, he was able to cut away the flesh which was hooked by the barb, and with more tugging and cutting it eventually came out. With great relief, he flopped down on the settee and just lay there for a while, trying not to move anything, to finally get rid of the waves of nausea which had plagued him throughout the ordeal.

At last he felt sufficiently recovered, as the responsibility of the boat nagged him into getting topside for a check. A short survey showed that all was okay; the autopilot was doing a superb job. *Thanks again, Dad, for that one.* Originally, David thought it was kind of dumb to have such a thing when there were people around to steer, but his dad was thinking of safety, and of long voyages yet unplanned.

He looked down at the small puncture on his shoulder, just now beginning to ooze more blood. Iodine—that was the treatment he had always gotten for his scraped knees and small cuts and, as much as he hated its sting, he knew it was good stuff. *At least then you knew you'd gotten something!* Into the medicine cabinet in the head he went, and found the vile-colored bottle. A little dab and—"Damn!"—the stuff had done its worst.

Tetanus shot! the words automatically jumped out. For this sort of thing that was part of the standard treatment. *But how can I get a shot, for cripes' sake?* Well, he'd just have to do without. Besides, after being dragged through the salty seawater for an hour or so, and then the fish, the hook should be clean anyway. Satisfied with this illogic, David turned his attention to other matters, such as that object ahead, bobbing nearly under the surface.

It was hard to locate, but he finally spotted the brown shape again. Immediately, he altered course to approach it, and in a short time it was just off the starboard bow. It now became apparent what the sodden bulk was. "Square grouper," he muttered, as the burlap-covered bale of marijuana drifted by, rolling gently with one corner breaking the surface, in a bobbing motion.

Kids he met from other boats in Georgetown told him about

these, named after the large groupers which lurked in coral grottoes, and were eagerly sought by fishermen, locals, and foreigners. It was at a beach barbeque on nearby Stocking Island that he heard about the drug bundles. At first, he thought they were pulling a snipe-hunt type of gag, but after several had related their stories of finding the square bales floating at sea, and some of even trying to open them, he believed it.

The best thing to do, they said, was to get far away from there, as soon as possible, because it meant that they had been dumped to escape detection before a boat was searched by the Coast Guard, or was to be picked up according to plan by someone nearby—especially if it were cocaine instead of hash inside. One way or the other, you didn't want to get in the way of whoever came; those guys killed without batting an eye. Boats get pirated all the time, so the stories went on; they just blast the owners away, take the boat to a pick-up point to load up, then smuggle the stuff into the U.S. mainland, disguised as yachties. Afterwards, they simply abandon the boat when they're done… or get caught. One way or the other, you're dead. Remember the notices put up on the post office bulletin board, by people trying to locate their friends and their boats? And on and on the stories went, into the night.

David was glad when his bale finally faded out of sight.

10

David steadily made progress through that day, toward the Turks and Caicos Islands group. According to his calculations, he should be sighting land in the next day or so. Then he could contact the authorities, Coast Guard or whoever about searching for his dad. With the prospect of help coming soon, he began to feel pleased with his accomplishment thus far. *Dad would be proud of at least that much,* he consoled himself.

Truthfully, he started to wonder what it was that he had fought about so much all these years, when it came to taking any initiative in learning to sail. All you do is put the sails up, point the boat in the right direction, and off you go. Simple! *If only Mom had been along on their first cruises, instead of Rachel,* the thought nagged at him.

But he was in too good a mood to ponder such ill-defined questions, and he set about preparing an early but super dinner. He dug into the refrigerator and found some steaks in the small freezer compartment—ah, just the thing. And a pineapple for that tropical touch. And… *A-ha, what's this?* The champagne his dad had bought, to break out the night after reaching the Virgin Islands. *Ah, well, what the hell.* Tomorrow he should be at Providenciales Island anyway, and he placed the bottle in a more accessible corner.

Soon, he had the charcoal broiler set up topside and the coals glowing red. In a short time, both steaks—he decided the other one wouldn't keep, anyway—were sizzling with a delicious aroma, and a faint trail of smoke drifted out over the stern, with the fading wake of the boat.

But, even with his rising enthusiasm for the meal, the nagging thought that his dad should be here to enjoy it with him ate away at him, and almost made him toss everything overboard. It was supposed to be a celebration marking the end of the trip, so what right did he have to eat and drink it all now? He was a failure—at making his dad proud, at sailing the boat, at being a good son, at… at… He stood transfixed with indecision, barbeque tongs in hand, not knowing where his feelings should be—where his loyalty should be.

The smell of the broiling steaks grew stronger. *Well, what would Dad tell me?* rambled through his mind. Dad hated to waste anything, so throwing it overboard wouldn't please him, for sure.

What about the reward angle? Would his dad think he had been doing good enough to earn a little reward by now? Certainly, his dad liked to give him rewards for his attempts at sailing, swimming, and other classes David felt he had been pushed into. *So, maybe this is like that, too: a reward. Plus not being wasteful.*

A drift of wind brought the steak odor his way again. David slowly reached over to turn one steak, then the other.

And, truly, the steaks were delicious—both of them. One he had cooked his regular way, well-done and without sauce, and the other had ample soakings of teriyaki sauce, plus a few dashes of Worcestershire. The pineapple picked up locally in the Exumas was just ripe and, true to that variety, not overly sweet.

By the time he was on his third large glass of bubbly, David finally felt that he had indeed had enough to eat. And perhaps too much to drink. But, after all, *This is a celebration, and at such times one is allowed to sin a little.* He chuckled at the thought.

Boy, if my friends could see me now, I'd be the envy of all those bastards! he thought, as he started to fill his fourth glass. Changing his mind, he opted for the bottle instead, and took a long swig.

Looking around at the passing sea and feeling the roll of the boat, he noticed that things weren't quite right, but never attributed it to the bottle in his hand. The bubbles caught him wrong as he swallowed, and he fairly exploded in a sneezing, coughing fit. Getting things under control once again, he broke out laughing aloud—then, just as suddenly, realized he had to take a leak before he burst.

Standing up at the railing, he unzipped his fly and prepared to let go. The lurching of the boat, combined with his unsteadiness, convinced his foggy mind that such a position was not the safest, and he'd better use the toilet in the head below. After having achieved that goal, he then settled into finishing what he could of the bottle.

David had been high on booze before, and even a few short trips on some mild hash, but that had all been limited excursions into that illicit zone of experience—usually at someone's party (with the parents worriedly trying to keep an eye on all the kids), or in a car outside a school dance (the challenge being to get out and then back in the building before the chaperones noticed). There were always other people around, and usually the supply was rather short, too. But, now…

Well, I'm Cock of the Rock, King of the Mountain, Captain of the Endeavor—this is different. He wasn't just any sniveling little teenager sneaking stuff out of his parents' liquor cabinet now. No, sir, he was legitimate; almost—sure, why not—an adult. *After all, didn't I succeed in getting this baby going, figuring it out for myself? And now I'm bringing it into safety, so that Dad…*

And then he ran out of congratulations.

The memory once again loose, he dipped into the depths of recriminations, hating himself for being such a brat, a poor learner, a miserable son. Yes, a miserable son even for Rachel. *After all,* he sloppily took yet another long swig, *what has she ever done to me?*

His eyes filled with tears, not so much out of compassion for Rachel, but for himself, being a poor divorced-family kid. And he wept with sympathy for his misfortune. He fairly wallowed in self-pity.

The last thing he remembered before passing out was that he was taking an oath to do something better next time, though he couldn't remember a stitch as to what it was.

The sea was kind to David that night; the wind slowly died and with it so did the waves, somewhat. By about 4:00 a.m. there was no wind at all, and the sails were slating about and raising such a clamor that even the almighty master of the vessel was awakened.

He made it through, releasing the sheets and halyards before he had to retch overboard. Again and again he vomited, until he felt he would die, and was making all sorts of resolutions regarding drink, as clearly as his foggy brain would let him form the concepts.

At last, the nausea was gone for a while, and he managed to get the sails sufficiently tied down, so the clanging of metal and rope would stop ringing in his head. Then he fell asleep again.

11

The sun beat intensely upon the sprawled figure in the cockpit. The wind had died completely, and the seas were confused as they tossed the water's surface into small peaks, which headed nowhere except up and down. The mast leaned precariously from one side to the other, as the boat rolled from side to side and rocked up and down, all at the same time.

As David awoke, he couldn't focus on exactly where he was and what was going on. It seemed as though nothing made any sense; he couldn't even raise himself straight to look around. That last failure was a serious mistake, because the lingering effects of his stomach's reaction last night now joined with real seasickness, and he was up over the rail again.

No resolutions this time (he couldn't remember last night's, anyway); just hanging on with grim determination, to wait for his churning stomach to settle down. An hour later, he was finally able to eat some crackers and sit upright.

Settling into the cockpit, David took an unsteady look around. He watched with odd fascination as the waves peaked and fell. The heat was stifling without any wind, and even in his distraught condition David was able to realize that this was new and somehow unusual. He couldn't escape the sense of suffocation anywhere above deck, as he shifted about from place to place beneath the cockpit dodger, then out onto the deck.

In desperation, he staggered below and fell onto a settee, panting and sweating profusely. This was no better. Indeed, it was worse for his stomach, and he struggled back up to the cockpit again.

While below, however, he did discover one foreboding fact: the barometer had dropped well into the *"Change"* zone, and seemed determined to fall even further. The sky remained a clear blue overhead, except a thin veil of high haze seemed to be coming from the northwest.

As David continued to look in that direction, a dark bank of clouds slowly rose from the horizon, seeming to spring up as though pushed by some invisible hand. Slight breezes began to play tag about the sea's surface, first from one direction and then another, skittering about like trapped mice before an approaching cat. David began to feel like one of the mice.

He knew something was coming, but exactly what he couldn't tell. Regardless, with this strange feeling in the air, and the sky looking so angry, he knew it couldn't be anything he'd like. *I'd better prepare, just in case. But, how?*

Usually in bad sailing weather—what little of it his family had experienced—David stayed below, out of the wind and rain, while his father handled the boat. So, he didn't even have that image to fall back on. But he at least knew that having too much sail up would be bad. So, the idea was to reef down and get the area reduced. His mind began to clear.

He knew there was something called a storm jib aboard, since he had once asked his dad what was in that sail bag they never opened. Well, it would be a start. A glance at the advancing murkiness on the horizon made him hustle. In short order, he dug out the never-used sail and unclipped the working jib from the forestay. Once it was stowed in a bag, he set about attaching the very stiff storm jib to the stay. It was made of extra heavy material and was exceedingly difficult to get on. But it was a small sail—almost ridiculously so, David thought, as he stepped back to look at it, hanging there like a wrinkled piece of sheet metal.

The air now turned suddenly cooler, and a light breeze was beginning from the northwest. *It's on its way.* With new urgency,

David carried the bagged jib back to the cockpit, threw it in, and attacked the main.

He knew the mainsail had something called reef points: rows of short lines dangling down, by which the sail could be made smaller. They were always there on the sail, but he had never paid much attention. Since the sail was already tied to the boom, and with the wind picking up rapidly, David didn't feel he had the leisure to learn something new.

Tossing the bagged jib down below, he followed to stow it and put away things which were loose and might spill. Halfway finished with that task, he felt a cold gust of air flush down the open companionway hatch, and the boat heeled hard over, as the front of the storm rolled upon them.

Losing his balance, David fell heavily into the settee, and sharply knocked his elbow against the lockers above, as he tried to save himself. Pots and pans clanged as they hit the floor, and slid to the leeward side. An open can of orange juice flew to the floor and went gurgling along, leaving a bright trail. Elsewhere, books and something which clumped loudly in his cabin also fell onto the floor. David struggled to get up and climb the ladder to the cockpit. The sight he witnessed fairly froze him…

All along the northwest horizon was a boiling, blue-black cloud which stretched for miles, and piled increasingly higher into the sky. It arched up over the water like a vacuum cleaner, scooping everything in its path. And, at the point where the cloud met the horizon, there no longer was any horizon. Instead, it was a frothy mixture of wind-driven spume and newly-born waves, cresting and crashing as soon as they rose.

The first gust preceding the dark mass, which heeled the boat over, never let up, and the small boat laid over at a sickening angle, for what seemed like forever to David. In moments, the full force was on him.

He struggled at the wheel to get the boat under control, his effort finally began to take effect, and the angle lessened. But now he was in for it, and he held on tight to the wheel, with a white-knuckled grip.

The first twenty minutes were the worst. That was when the wind was highest—over 45 knots—and the rain came in stinging curtains to whip against his face. That's what he hadn't expected: the rain. It came down by the tons. Never in his wildest imaginings had he conceived of anything like the dense sheets of water, wave after wave of it, completely blocking out all sight, and forcing him to steer only by the feel of the wind on his soaked back.

He was running before the wind now, steering just slightly off downwind, to let the following waves slide safely beneath and not take control, twisting the boat sideways. He had seen his dad do that before, in much milder conditions, and was now thankful for the memory.

After the wind abated somewhat, he began to look around. The main squall line was now a less distinct entity, as it moved on past him. However, despite the general lightening of the sky and increased visibility, the wind was still high and the seas tumbling—not as bad as before, but still suspicious. As his glance moved to the boat, his eyes riveted on the deck. The front hatch was partly open; he had forgotten to close it amidst all the excitement. "Oh, shit!" he spit the words out.

He knew that a mess awaited him below. The hatch was directly over the bunk in his cabin. *Damn, why don't I learn?* he chastised himself further. *Dad always made me check my cabin when we expected heavy weather, and I fought his insisting. What a fool! Now that Dad isn't here, I've got to remember to do it myself. I've got to remember everything!* And anger from the frustration welled within him.

Leaving the steering to the autopilot for a few moments, he dashed below. Indeed, his cabin was a royal mess. Everything was soaked, and what wasn't soaked was thrown all over. But he didn't have time right then to clean it up, so he closed the hatch and tightened the latches, grabbed a few dry clothes, and shut the door on the whole heap.

Back in the cockpit, all his attention was now devoted to keeping the boat under control. He had by now abandoned all hope of maintaining his original course; his dinner party last night had seen to that, since he had lost track of time and direction during the night—two very necessary quantities for dead reckoning.

But I'd better come up with some kind of chart position, he realized, as the strain of his task began to wear, and did a quick GPS reading to plot on the chart. He glanced at the rolling compass card and, after a few moments, was able to determine an average heading from the gyrations. Noting the time and direction, David felt better about his navigation. It was an extremely rough calculation, but it was better than nothing; at least it gave him some sense of control over what was happening.

And so the day wore on. In periods of slightly calmer wind— the half-hour lull before a renewed blast of air descended—he was able to use the autopilot and leave the wheel to relieve himself, or get something to eat. Running before the wind is not an autopilot's best point of sail, so it was with heightened apprehension that he let it take over, as he hustled about his chores.

By nightfall, it was apparent that conditions were not going to let up, and he began to worry about what to do. He obviously couldn't steer all night. The boat was barely under control now, and he was getting very tired. He struggled hard with the logic of the situation, trying to make the pieces fit with what he remembered his dad doing or saying. Or even fit with movies he had seen on television—the old ones, where famous movie stars were cast as pirate captains or misfits of the South Seas, on leaky old trading schooners. What was it they did during those horrendous scenes of hurricanes and typhoons?

Finally, an amalgamation of it all resulted in… "Bare poles," he muttered, as the words from his brief reading about sailing

safety flashed to mind. He'd take down his last sail and just let
the boat take care of itself; as long as it floated, he would be okay.
In truth, there was little else he could do, he admitted, as he set
about getting the storm jib down, while scenes of Tyrone Power
struggling at the spoked wheel of a square-rigger in pouring rain
faded from reality.

In the movies, of course, somebody was standing just off-set
throwing buckets of water and squirting hoses. He conjured up
the image jokingly, as he finally unsnapped the last hank and
started stuffing the storm jib in its bag. *I'm living the real thing.* And
that last thought brought some warmth of consolation, which
somehow helped.

With the sail gone and the wheel tied to bring the boat
somewhat into the wind, it was certainly rougher, as the boat
heeled far over one way and back again with each cresting wave.
But David found he could adjust to the new rhythm. He took an
average of the general direction of their drift, due to the wind,
noted it on the chart, and wedged himself into his father's aft
bunk, where there wasn't much space to be thrown around.

He hadn't really been in the cabin, so to speak, since that first
night of discovery. He had stepped in to get a few tools or
whatever, but he never stayed long. It was like there was
something in there—a persistent presence which made David
feel very uncomfortable, if not outrightly afraid. But now he had
little choice. His cabin was a disaster and, besides, this was the
place with the least motion to it.

Yet, more than that, David had begun to feel less estranged
from the cabin. The more success he had with his efforts to sail
the boat, the more he felt as though he had a right to be there. It
was a strange feeling, like when he was steering at the wheel that
other night, when he felt he wasn't himself. And it wasn't really
as though he was trying to fill his father's shoes, either. It was
himself, alright, but he was growing inside, with his skin about
to burst and someone struggling to come out. It was like

someone or something being born—not new, but more like renewed.

The concept and feeling seemed intensely familiar to David, as though he'd had the feeling before, and that there were steps or realms of experience beyond this, which he had also attempted but was not ready for. Or… something. He couldn't figure it out, but it was disturbing. Not disturbing in the sense of anguish, but as a sort of yearning, a seeking of something familiar which is desired very much; a right that one is entitled to. Being in his father's cabin made him feel that way. Still, David knew there was more beyond that simple fact.

But he was too exhausted to carry the burdensome thoughts any further, and he soon succumbed to the demands of his body…

And the shapeless dream mists slid stealthily into the cabin, and quickly floated him off on billowing clouds, to continue the challenge of his illusive slumberland quest.

12

All that night and the next day, the wind blew from a northwesterly direction. David didn't bother attempting to get any sail up. It was still blowing 25-30 knots, plus regular gusts well beyond that—and, besides, he didn't feel so great. The aftermath of his celebration proved to be no preparation for what he had to endure in those next days, so he just crawled from his bunk to the galley, the head, and back again, existing in a dreamy state of semi-consciousness, which sufficed to make the time go faster.

During the second night, the wind finally fell to a more normal 13-18 knots, then veered north toward the east, as the trade winds once again established their customary pattern.

When David crawled up the companionway ladder the following morning, a beautiful sight greeted him: the big blue bowl was once again overhead, a burning sun was drying out the wet decks, and the swells from Africa rolled in endless hills and valleys, for as far as he could see.

And that vision brought yet another surprise, and he quickly scrambled up to stand on the cabin top, to get a better view. *I can't believe it! An island!*

Or, at least he thought it was. Then it disappeared.

As the boat rose to the crest of another swell, David strained hard to see. And there it was again; it definitely was an island! *The binoculars!* He tore below and was instantly back with them crammed to his eye. Not just one island, but two… or more.

Or just one that's all broken up? Anyway, it's land! Glorious land—

something solid to stand on once again! And, as he thought this, his animosities against the sea and his situation rose to squash some of the newly sprouted affections for boat and sea. Old roots are hard to kill.

But he'd never get there drifting about like this. They were just to the south, and he would miss them completely at this rate. Besides, the wind was now rapidly shifting to come from the direction he wanted to be going. Quickly he set to his task, his mind reeling off footage of scenes which might be found: beaches, palm trees, coconuts, parrots, a calm lagoon (blessed peace!), and... yes, even a sarong-clad native girl, rushing to greet him with a lei.

The more he imagined, the faster he worked, and suddenly he was done. Almost startled, he stood dumbly staring at his preparations for a moment, then leapt into the cockpit.

In short order, and with a confidence which even surprised him, the boat was underway and on course: the tall mainsail tightly stretched out from the silver mast, as though the sail were chasing it, while the jib seemed to race on out ahead, pulling and urging them both onward. The bow dove and smashed into the waves, and white water poured, gurgling and seething, alongside. Ah, it was glorious to be alive, and David devoted his whole being to the broad grin that he now wore.

Yet, as he neared the islands, he could see it wasn't all that sweet. A frothy white ring seemed to go unbroken around his goal. Clearly, it had a reef around it, David sourly noted, as he once more descended into reality. *Where the hell am I, anyway...? The chart! Maybe it's on the chart,* the thought burst in, and he dashed below.

He hurriedly scanned it, taking out a set of parallel rulers, to try to establish a line of travel the boat may have been on. There seemed to be nothing that would fit this description between where he started a few days ago and the Turks and Caicos—nothing at all. He ran his finger along his assumed course again.

Nothing.

Then, his eyes went straight beyond his intended destination, and zeroed in on an irregular-colored area on the chart: "Silverado Bank", along with a few small dots named, "Thornbourne Group", he murmured the names. A large, flat area of shallow water, east of the Turks and Caicos.

East? Dumbfounded, he stared at the map and again retraced his assumed line of travel. There was no doubt; he had missed his intended landfall at Turks and Caicos completely. The storm had taken him right by them!

"Oh… my… god!" he muttered angrily. *That's where I was supposed to get help. Now what? Here I am and Dad's way back there.* He slowly ran his finger over the map. The distance was staggering. *How…? What…?*

He couldn't finish the pressing questions, which arose with the clenching emotions now starting to consume his body and mind. Despair and recrimination popped out from their lairs, where David thought he had managed to confine them—at least, for a while. But they were not to win the battle. A body and mind, whatever the age, cannot tolerate such an assault, again and again, without building defenses. And so it was with David.

After fighting welling tears and a tightening chest, he began to win the battle for control.

"Okay," he said aloud, in a strained voice, as he wiped away the few tears that reached his line of defense, "I can do this." He paused. *Now, what would Dad do? What would he want me to do?* His mind went back to the comforting questions which had served him well thus far, seeking his father's advice.

Gregory was not stoic, nor immune to emotion, and was aware of its role in certain situations of decision-making. However, logic and reasoning were his primary tools for figuring out what should be done in most cases—especially those which are bound by time and need for action, when you have to be realistic about what is possible. He always believed that was what made him a good sailor, because sailing is full of those situations of making decisions, and he hoped some of that viewpoint would be absorbed by his son.

David slowly rolled the situation over in his mind, again and again. *I'm here and Dad's back there. Can I sail back to the Turks?*

And, honest thoughts about his skills and fears raised their faces, without masks hiding the truth.

No…

Well, I just don't know. What if I end up needing help, too… because of something stupid I do, or just can't do? That takes more time from Dad to get help. That didn't sound too good to David.

So, how else can I get help? A good question. If he couldn't go back, for lots of reasons, then: *What's in the other direction—forward?* And he returned to the map.

He quickly scanned from where he was, close to the Thornbourne Group, then onward from there. The massive island of the Dominican Republic was to the south. He knew nothing about it, which was a sort of intimidating feeling. Farther beyond that was Puerto Rico, which he had at least heard of before, and knew that it was part of the U.S. somehow—not so scary.

"So, what do I do?" he asked his dad again. And, after a few moments' thought: *Well, I can't get to either place right now; these islands are in the way. I need to do some planning and get things ready, and get some courage up.* He didn't know if he could even sail it. *So far, it's all been mostly downwind and being blown around, to be honest.*

He stood frozen with indecision, but one of his dad's past lectures finally popped to mind. *What's done is done; you can't redo the past. Get safe first, then figure out the rest later.*

He had to act now. The growing sight of the surf pressed him to stare more closely at his new landfall—if he could get in. There didn't seem to be another chart which had the small, out-of-the-way islands on it, so David was forced to conclude what he could from this one.

Well, he thought quickly, *this is probably a lot like what Dad explained about the Bahamian banks.* Shallow, sandy plateaus rising steeply out of the Atlantic depths, with small limestone islands, shoals, or coral reefs along the edge.

David had hardly acknowledged Gregory's instruction then, but now it made sense. "There's always a break through somewhere," his dad had said; "it's just a matter of finding it."

And now, on the northeast edge of the bank, near the group of islands, the chart seemed to show such a break—at least, the depth contour lines on the paper weren't continuous there.

Probably a mistake by the guy drawing it, David bitterly mused, *distracted by a pretty girl in the office or something. But that's all I got to go on, so let's take a look.* He swung the boat to intercept the faintly marked, broken line.

As David drew closer, it became apparent that there indeed was more than one island. Just how many was impossible to tell but, whatever the number, it made a rather confusing appearance. Since his heading was north of the group, he was able to come in at an angle, which would intercept at the one end. Then as he turned, he would be able to cruise along their length, just outside the reefs, and get a better idea of what dangers were there. If he spotted an opening elsewhere, he could duck in at that point, instead.

As he made his approach, David could finally make out what appeared to be five separate islands, with several small islets scattered among the larger, rugged ones. Several had cliffs perhaps seventy feet in height, broken sharply in places, so they seemed to almost fall straight into the water. Others were more regularly shaped, tapering off to flattened ends, which disappeared gradually into the water as sandy beaches. All were heavily vegetated by brush and small trees, with a few coconut palms in clumps near the beaches.

The fringing reef rose sharply out of the dark blue depths and was capped by a continuous froth of breaking swells, behind which was the lighter blue color of shallow lagoons and white sand banks. But nowhere could he see a break. Off in the far distance, along the bank, he thought there were fewer breakers, but not close to where he assumed the break should be.

Then he saw it: a short distance of dark blue water, which extended into the bank between the heavily breaking seas. There were rollers there, too, but not always breaking like the reef sides. He stared hard at the water and, as far as he could determine, there were no obstructing coral heads or sand bores across the entrance. This had to be it.

"Let's do it," he murmured huskily, to inspire self-confidence, and immediately he swung the boat toward the opening, gripping the wheel tightly, as the wind filled the sails and heeled the boat hard over on the new tack. The small craft surged forward and rushed toward the opening.

As they approached closer, the growing strength of the swells, while they raked the steeply rising bottom, immediately felt like a grasping hand, as David struggled to maintain control. It seemed as though he were flying, with the wind sucking at the sails and the steepening rollers pushing from behind. He was committed now; there was no turning back.

And finally, with first a giant slide down one wave and then a huge boost from another, they were through. Just like that. Immediately the seas calmed, and the sails again assumed command. David steered his little ship over diminishing waves, until only a light chop roughened the water's surface.

A big breath of air and tightened muscles suddenly loosened… he hadn't realized how tense he had been! *Well, we made it—that's what counts.*

And now he switched his total interest to the islands.

He had to beat his way back upwind a tack or two, just like in sailing school, but it was a short distance. They were soon in the lee of the islands and the winds diminished, becoming fluky in their intention. He finally had to drop the sails altogether; they coasted for a bit, then stopped.

David stared out at his surroundings, amazed in no small way at the significance of where he now was. He had made it on his own this far, even after all his many faulty decisions, because of several good ones he had made as well.

Dad would be proud, he mused out of habit, and then remembered. The pressing recent memories soured his feeling of accomplishment somewhat, but did not spoil it completely. *No, Dad would be proud!* he emphatically thought again. That's something David was sure of.

And, now, what of the rescue plan? Dad had said to get safe first and figure out the rest later. Well, he was safe now—at least as far as he could tell. Figuring out the plan to get help in the Dominican Republic or Puerto Rico was next on the list.

13

But that was hard to focus on. *It's been... how long since Dad disappeared now? Five, six days?* It seemed like it had been forever, and his dislike for dredging up those memories and questions forced it all farther away from a clear reality in his mind. *Later. I'll face that later.*

"Take things in order of need," his dad always reminded David, when he was confused about what to do first. Well, now he needed some rest and recuperation, before he tackled the rescue problem.

Besides, he had just arrived at this apparent bit of Heaven, and that was pulling his attention strongly to the affairs of the moment—away from the past and future needs, to the mysteries of his immediate environment.

He was behind one of the islands, with a cliff rising just slightly taller than his mast. The cliff genuinely wasn't all that high, but coming abruptly from the water it gave the appearance of being very high. On either side, the land fell off at a slight angle and eventually ran into the lagoon—at least, the west end did; he couldn't see where the east end went, since it was behind yet another, similar island.

There seemed to be a passage between the two, with other islands in the background. As a whole, the entire scene gave the appearance of being a maze, with the light blue water of the lagoon providing pathways among the gray-green island blocks. None of the islands were over a mile long, it seemed, but they appeared big, because of the sheerness of their height. There were also the flatter ones he had seen briefly from offshore.

It was confusing, but there was time enough to straighten that out. Right now, all David wanted to do was get ashore and feel some of that solid earth, once again. In short order, he had the anchor down, launched the inflatable dinghy, and was motoring toward the nearest island.

This, the westernmost of the group, started with a low, sandy beach, then climbed up in a series of humps, until the cliff was reached. Then it fell stairstep, in tumbled blocks of gray limestone, toward another island, similarly constructed. Behind those two seemed to be jagged islets, scattered through a passageway leading to three more large islands beyond.

Later, David thought. The first order of the day was to get two feet on some beautiful solid ground—or at least a beach, since that seemed to be the only available place to avoid the rocky, wave-worn shoreline. He headed directly toward the eastern point, opening up the throttle on his little outboard, until its sharp bark echoed off the cliffs.

Cutting the throttle, the noise stopped and he coasted gently to shore, with the backwash of his dinghy. He slowly lowered one foot, then the other, and pulled the inflatable up onto the beach. Taking out an oar, he solemnly marched above the tide line and dramatically planted it blade-up in the sand. "I hereby claim this land for… ME!" He shouted the last word and burst out laughing.

He whooped and took off, running hard, throwing little spurts of sand from his feet into the air as he went. He knew he was being silly, but… *But, damn it, I'm happy—very happy!* He felt he had earned a little reprieve from having to be responsible and grown-up. So, he tore around the beach, until he finally halted in exhaustion, bending over with hands on knees and gasping for breath. Recovering, he finally looked up and made a closer appraisal of his discovered land.

It wasn't quite the tropic isle he had envisioned when

offshore. Thick underbrush covered nearly every square foot of the surface above the beach. Some of the bushy plants were large enough to be called trees, and there were a few coconut palms, but the rest formed an almost impenetrable mass of intertwined branches, roots, and leaves.

Everything was very dry, not lush and green as in the movies. The sun was scorching, and seemed determined to not let live anything which wasn't cloaked in thorns or heavy bark. Only some parched grasses from an earlier rainy season looked familiar to David. Wandering lines of stubby mangrove sprigs poked out of the sand, tracing the roots spreading from the mother plant, back at the edge of the bush. The steep, jumbled rock hills were likewise clad by brush, wherever there was an indentation in the rock to allow a little water to collect.

But it wasn't without its beauty. Just the setting—the wildness of it all amidst the sparkling water—was something worth seeing, he had to admit. Moreover, many of the bushes bore bright red flowers and small, round, greenish-purple fruit, which must have provided food for the several kinds of birds flitting from bush to bush, arguing over territorial rights or singing a song, seemingly just for pleasure. These bits of color and sound made the place less unfriendly to David.

No, it certainly wasn't what he had expected, but it was land, and someplace to escape from the demands of the sea—a place to play and be a kid again for a little longer, before having to assume the mantle of captain and adult once again.

And so he played, for what was left of the day.

The next morning, when David climbed to the cockpit of his anchored boat, he heard a strange sound, quickly becoming louder. It was a pulsing sound, sort of like the drumming of a grouse he and his dad had once heard, during a hike in a forest.

Except this was steady… mechanical. Suddenly, a boat appeared from behind one of the islands, heading toward him.

What…? He was confused, but quickly became heartened. *People! Maybe some help!*

As the shabby island fishing boat came closer, David raised his arm and waved. They didn't slow down. He started to jump up and down as well, and gesture toward his boat. Finally, the boat turned and slowed down, coming close, and stopped.

"Hey," David called out. The pulsing engine was too loud, even at idle. "Can you turn off your motor?" He went through a series of gestures to indicate what he wanted. After a few moments, one of the two men aboard smiled broadly, popped into a doorway then back out, as the engine coughed and stopped.

"Hey, how're you doing?" David spoke loudly. They were still a bit far, but close enough to converse, he figured.

The two men smiled and waved. "Hey, mon," the shorter man called out, "we doin' good. How you doin'?"

"Okay, I'm doing okay." *Now what do I say…? Just chat a little.* "I'm just taking a little rest here. What're you guys doing here?"

The short one spoke to the taller man, who evidently didn't know English. Tall One smiled and nodded at David. "We on our way to fishing place… down that way," Short One gestured toward the east. "We fishermen," he proudly announced.

"Hey, that's good. Do you catch lots of fish?"

"Yeah, mon. We good fishermen. Make lots of money." Smiling, he translated to Tall One, who broke into a big grin and tapped his proud chest, then gestured as if to count money in his hand.

David laughed broadly with them and continued, "Where are you coming from?" *It's time to ask the questions.*

"We come from Cockburn Town."

"Where's that?"

Short One looked at Tall One and smiled. "Caicos. We from

Caicos."

"Oh. I've never been there." *Sort of a dumb thing to say.* "Well, when did you leave there?"

Short One translated.

"We leave yesterday."

Okay, so maybe… But how to ask? "Hey, did you hear any news about somebody being found in the sea? Like, maybe they fell off a boat?" *Not very clear, but maybe they'll get the idea.*

More translating. Talking.

"I don't know… What you mean?"

David paused and began again, slowly. "I mean, maybe somebody was rescued from the sea after falling off a boat, over toward the Bahamas? Did you hear anything like that?" It was out now, and a jumble of feelings and memories bounced around in his mind. He watched the men talk and gesture to each other.

Suddenly, Short One smiled and called out, "My friend heard a man was found. Maybe… four days ago." He turned and patted Tall One on the shoulder.

David's heart took a few leaps. "Was he alive?" *Aargh, another terrible question. But I gotta know…*

Short One translated again. A bit of a disagreement seemed to be going on. He turned back to David. "My friend say he was alive. He sure."

"Was he American?" *What else?* "Uh, was he white or a local man?" *God, what a thing to have to ask, but I need more details.*

A quick discussion on the fishing boat. "My friend say he don' know." The two men looked a little restless, but were still polite.

A new question popped up: "Do you have a radio on the boat?" A new hope.

Short One turned to his friend, and they both grinned at the absurdity of the question. He gave a quick answer: "No, we got no radio. We not rich."

David didn't know what more to ask.

"Hey, mon, we got to go; long trip to fishing place." And he showed a broad grin. Tall One joined in.

"Okay. Hey, thanks for the info. I was just curious." *What else?* "I hope you have a good fishing trip," David smiled widely, mimicking their mood.

He watched as they started the engine, waving as they moved off and picked up speed. In short order, they were out of sight.

And David was alone again.

14

"Now what?" David mumbled, as he turned to stare at his surroundings. He was sort of nestled between two of the islands, and on the channel which seemed to lead between them all. *Probably as good a place to be anchored as any,* he concluded, and checked to see that the anchor was safely sunk into the sandy bottom. He could easily see the chain from it leading up to *Endeavor*'s bow, seemingly suspending the boat in the air, since the water was so clear.

The boat was motionless upon the glassy waters between the scattered islands, which blocked much of the wind from the northeast. Terns were busy flying overhead, however, calling with a raucous screech at each other, as they dipped into the sea for food, then fought in aerial acrobatics for custody of whatever anyone found.

In the scrub brush and trees, he could distantly hear songbirds singing out the boundaries of space each claimed, and chasing trespassers onto the next territory, where they would again be assailed. Though he saw nothing on the ground, he assured himself that there was undoubtedly a hidden activity of animal life proceeding there, too. Everyone was busy… except David.

Yet his mind was active, trying to figure out what to do with the information the fishermen provided. Slowly, he again turned to his father as a model. *Dad is pretty good at logically thinking stuff out,* he had to conclude, as he bounced over a smattering of memories, where his dad proved right in so many cases regarding David's activities. Though he didn't like to admit it, his dad was usually right—lately, David had little reluctance about facing that fact.

Alright, let's figure this out like Dad would. They said that a man was pulled from the sea four days ago. So, that timing would fit. They couldn't say if he was white or local. Well, that's something that could be lost when the information was sent to the police, or whoever; those things happen, he concluded.

Tall One seemed to be rather certain that somebody pulled a man out of the water, and that he was alive. *The tall guy was arguing pretty seriously, too, raising his voice and waving his arms around. He looked like he knew what he was talking about,* David convinced himself, and felt good about it. *Alive!* He let a small smile creep in.

No radio. That was quite disappointing, though David could see from the men's reactions—as well as the fishing boat's condition and their clothes—why they laughed. *A pretty stupid question, but I had to ask. It would have been great, but...* And so that door was closed.

"Not bad," he announced, as he finished going over the conversation and its implications. He felt quite good about it all, even though there were some things he wished they had known, or that he could have asked. But the main thing was that a man had been found, and he was alive—and it fit the time frame for his journey thus far. He felt good about all of that and sat in the cockpit for a while, as the rest of the inhabitants of the island world continued their lives, without regard for his.

Gradually, though, he realized he was still stuck with the question "What now?" To his regret, it didn't go away; it still hovered over his head, like a crown of thorns rather than a halo.

Decisions—I hate them! Well... sometimes I don't, he had to admit. *But why can't I just go... and play? And not have to worry about these...* he couldn't find the word, but finally did, *...adult things that Dad always dealt with...?*

And, bingo! He glimpsed flashes of insight into what was going on—what was going on during this whole trip. Why his dad wanted him to go on it; what he had to do now and forever in the future. To learn to make decisions. To simply grow up.

And growing up is something everyone does, always. There's no end to it, because there are always decisions to be made, and being an adult means facing that fact and figuring it out, not giving up and crying. That's what a kid does.

I gotta face the decision. I gotta do it. That's what Dad does, and I have to, too… He paused, brain-weary. *But, damn, it's hard,* he grimaced.

A particularly noisy flock of screeching terns circled the boat, as they wheeled and fought over a small fish, which dropped from someone's beak into the water. The flurry of action distracted David and, eventually, his growling stomach joined the chorus of the fray. He got up, slid down to the galley, and opened a food locker.

Later that evening, on a full tummy, he felt he was ready to face the question. *Okay, lay it out; get the facts out.*

First, he had earlier decided to go to the D.R. or Puerto Rico for help. That still made sense, regardless of anything else. He still needed help with the boat—what to do with it afterward, if nothing else. Also, he still had a lot to learn about sailing, especially on the open sea. *That's a given. I just have to figure out when.*

And then there were the fishermen. According to them, his dad was apparently pulled from the sea and alive… somewhere. He smiled at the thought and bathed in the relief it brought. Yet, running back over the encounter and the conversation, sprigs of doubt tried to break through that confidence.

They really seemed sure of what they said, even though it was a bit… hard to understand, because of the language difference, he reassured himself. Then he addressed another doubt: *I don't think they were just saying what I wanted to hear, either.* And that sprig was also pushed back down, but it lingered a bit longer.

Why would they want to lie to me? They seemed pretty honest to me. They were poor, but honest, I'm sure.

Having examined the truth of the information to his satisfaction, as his dad would have done, he enjoyed the relief which swept back over his body and mind.

Okay, great! Dad's alright someplace, so he's taken care of. I don't have to worry about him so much—nor feel so guilty. And that half-aware agony was pushed farther back into its cave.

I really don't know exactly where he is. It's a gamble to assume he's still in Turks and Caicos, waiting for me… So, I guess I sail on to one of those other places, maybe Puerto Rico.

But that wasn't such a great thing to look forward to. Yes, he was gaining confidence and skill in sailing; however, he had to admit that it still made him fearful, despite his limited success and bravado at times. *So, what should I do about that problem?*

His sailing school lessons came to mind. *What was the purpose of those, anyway? I could have just read books about sailing, so why go through it all?* More thinking: him out sailing, his dad watching, encouraging. Finally… *Oh! I get it.*

"Practice makes perfect, or at least makes you better," he realized, as his dad's words rang clear. *That's what I need to do: practice sailing.* Especially getting used to raising and lowering *Endeavor's* sails quickly and easily, until it was second nature to him.

But doubts still lingered, as memories of the past flooded in. *Okay, I'm still a little afraid of the water. What's above—like the wind and waves—as well as what's under… I mean, who knows what's there?*

More thinking. *So-o-o, I should spend some time practicing being on the water and under it. Practice on this big lake here. Get rid of my fears, then sail on. That makes sense. That's what Dad would decide,* he added confidently.

So, off to new adventures tomorrow! He allowed a big grin as he clambered into his bunk.

David slept well that night.

PART TWO

15

Exploring the rest of the islands for a few days, as a way to practice sailing, was one of his first adventures. And the islands proved to be a match for any young man's imaginings of pirates and Spanish galleons, with their intricate channels, cliff-top lookouts, eroded overhangs leading to short caves within, and a very snug little cove, which he eventually moved and wriggled *Endeavor* into.

This particular spot was just about in the middle of the island group, but sort of at one side, where a tall, spire-like islet almost butted up against the cliff of one of the islands, looking like it had all but been split off from it. It was impossible to see the opening from any distance, and one had to almost stumble upon it to find it, as he had. It was just deep enough to float the sloop at low water. *A perfect hideaway!* David thought, with relish.

Every kid, all through their youth, looks for the perfect secret place, for whatever purpose intended, and David grinned shamelessly every time he sailed or rowed out of the cove in the dinghy, on another day's exploration…

One of the islands just over from his cove had a special surprise for him. During the night, he had occasionally heard a strange sound as it wafted on the wind; it was a cacophony of chirpings, like birds squabbling, only not wild birds, but more something like chickens—or birds trying to crow like chickens.

One day, after a particularly still night, when the wind dropped to almost nothing, the chirping sounds kept him awake half the night. Now he was very curious, and the next morning he set out toward where he thought the sound originated.

Of course, not a chirp was to be heard anywhere. However, as he analyzed which direction the wind would carry the sound, he decided that it had to come from this one larger islet, which was brush-covered and had a sort of depression in its middle. At least, that's what it seemed to be from outward appearances, as he rowed toward it.

After a bit of searching, he managed to find a tiny beach, about twenty feet wide, on which to land. Having pulled the dinghy up, he stood for a moment or two to look around, then started to walk inland, wherever the brush would allow passage. It was hot and scarcely any air penetrated the cover.

It wasn't long before he started to notice curious markings on the ground, wherever there was sand or dirt: lines, which went snaking back and forth, as though something had been dragged. In some places, the ground was covered with the lines.

He had been right in guessing that there was a large depression in the middle of the island, because he very soon found himself having to descend, hand over hand, down a steep bank.

As he was doing so, at a particularly steep place, he was about to reach out to grasp a rock, when the rock moved! Then it just darted away in a flash. Startled, David froze where he was and looked intently about him. Another rock moved to his right, then another, and he finally realized what they were.

Iguanas. Huge lizards the color of the rocks, but with green or scarlet iridescence about their stubby heads, a pale pendulous throat pouch, and a ridge of short spines running down their backs and tails.

David gave a short gasp and jerked back quickly, forgetting that he was precariously perched on the bank. He slipped downward about ten feet, over loose rock, and came abruptly to a stop on the gnarled trunk of a small tree, which looked as though it had been clinging in its equally precarious position for hundreds of years. But it held.

Catching his breath and shuddering at the close encounter, David paused to look around. He was now where he could see into the depression, and what he saw equaled his initial reaction to the surprise a moment before.

There were seemingly hundreds of iguanas lying about the bare, cracked mud of the dried pond which formed the center of the depression. Most were just immobile, sunning themselves, or else slowly moving into and out of the encircling brush—like so many commuters about a city public transit station. A few squabbles were taking place here and there, but for the most part it was a very tranquil scene.

Then, what were they doing at night, to raise such a ruckus? The question nagged at David. *Probably getting high on cactus juice and partying all night*, he thought, as his imagination started rolling.

He had soon engineered an entire scenario of typical human party happenings, with groups singing old favorite tunes (out of key, of course), playboys trying to make it with eligible single girls, bosses getting overly friendly with secretaries, husbands and wives beginning the weekly argument, the party clown doing his thing, and the sexy little nymph doing hers—except that it was all these iguanas having the party, all night long, night after night after night.

A rustle behind him jerked David back from the party fantasy, to face one very large iguana, who didn't seem to be in the least intimidated by David's larger size. "Nice lizard. Nice iguana," David croaked, as he tried to edge off to his right. But, no sooner had he started in that direction than another iguana appeared, blocking the route, then another, and another. Soon, he had iguanas all about him.

Now, this is ridiculous. They're nothing but curious animals. Just lizards. Big ones, but still lizards, he reassured himself. But they weren't moving. Well, something had to give, and he yelled, "Yah!" and waved his arms.

All hell broke loose as iguanas fell, leapt and ran, every which way—including his. Some narrowly missed hitting him, as they scrambled in terror at this Gulliver, who had chanced upon their isle.

In ten seconds the dust had cleared, and all that was to be seen or heard was scurrying, receding into the bush—except for one *very* large specimen. He, she, whatever it was, stood stock still, staring at him. It wasn't four feet away, at about eye level.

David didn't move, either.

Then, turning its head slightly, so that one eye fixed upon David and presented the profile of its bulk, it paused for a moment then wallowed off into the bush, with that peculiar twisting-walking motion of lizards.

Having gotten the drift of that warning, David himself scurried off into the bushes, and never went back to that particular islet.

Every night, though, as he lay in his bunk, he would grin impishly, as the sounds of the iguana party drifted over the water.

16

While the lack of lush vegetation on the islands had been a disappointment to David, the profusion of life underwater was a complete surprise for his next adventure. Of course, he and his dad had done some snorkeling on small reefs, elsewhere in the Bahamas on the way down, but that experience was limited to shallow, poorly developed coral outcroppings. However, his initial dive the second day after arrival here was an event which would probably stand out forever in his list of memorable firsts.

David felt that he had come a long way in overcoming his childhood fear of monsters in the water, though much of the progress was made by shoving the idea into a far corner of his mind, rather than by facts and logic. But this technique sufficed, so he was able to enjoy his first experience with skin-diving last year in Florida, when they brought *Endeavor* down the Intracoastal Waterway. He wasn't immediately eaten by Jaws or attacked by moray eels, or anything else, except for some small, white fish along the water's edge, which nibbled on his toes as he stood hesitantly scanning the gentle waves lapping the sandy beach.

He eventually even forced himself to look at a diving book featuring pictures of sharks—the classic fear of all neophyte divers. He got to know the types fairly well—*Just in case,* he thought—and in truth found the book's following sections on coral reefs quite interesting, with their many fish, corals, plant life, and other myriad forms of creepy-crawlies. But he still wasn't prepared for what he found on these islands.

The reef he first chose was a branch of the islands' fringing reef, one which trailed off into the lagoon, like so many others, yet was still quite extensive and required a bit of maneuvering the dinghy to get into the middle of it. He could immediately see, through the breeze-ruffled surface, that it was much different from what he had seen before.

Broad yellow branches of staghorn coral spread just beneath the surface, and graced the tops of ridges which fell off to deep gullies, with white sand carpeting their floors. Enticing as it was, David was hesitant, then determined to overcome his old fears. He decided philosophically that the unknown would always control him, unless he made it known... and, with that, rolled off into the water.

Instantly it was another world, alive with fish swimming above and below him, and purple and yellow sea fans waving gently with the current. It was like waking up from a solid night's sleep, only to find that your bed is in the middle of a multi-story department store, during the after-Christmas sale.

He rose to the surface for a breath and looked about. A few seagulls were winging their way to some imagined food source, the water rippled slightly to disturb its otherwise monotonous flatness, a few puffy clouds drifted in a bright sky, and the dinghy bobbed gently on its anchor rode. Pretty quiet stuff. He lowered his head below... and the Christmas sale was on again.

Small fish—some brilliant blue, others dotted with crimson or yellow, with stripes or dots—hovered over the sale table of greenish-yellow brain corals, darting in and out of the convolutions, and looking for morsels yet unfound by their competitors.

Other corals were hovered over by fleets of striped butterflyfish or gaudy angelfish, with their long, trailing fins, all seeming to pose for each other, showing off their finery in vain attempts to keep others from the sales rack below. Triggerfish, with their pointed heads and worried, beady eyes, constantly rushed from coral to coral, unable to decide which was the best buy.

And, of course, the samplers were there, too: fat green and blue parrotfish, cruising from table to table, pushing in to nibble a bit of coral, then unconcernedly moving on to another. An occasional overweight grouper could be seen wiggling its large form out of one cave dressing-room, to see if anyone was watching, then darting back into another, to try on a different size. The whole scene was a riot to David, and he put this experience right up there with the iguanas' midnight party.

Becoming familiarized with it all, David also began to cruise over the Christmas sale offerings of the reef. Irrepressibly, he was pulled to examine the landscape more closely and started diving down—shallow at first, but as his breath-holding abilities increased he went deeper, sometimes to fifteen feet.

He saw several brown moray eels poking their sinuous bodies out of holes, their toothed mouths open—but he knew this was only how they breathed through their gills, so he resolved to just watch where he placed his hands, and didn't worry about the morays anymore. He quickly discovered that the reef was not solid, but a labyrinth of holes, tunnels, and caves, some quite large enough to allow his passage—but he wasn't ready for that yet.

Back in some of these holes, he could see reddish speckled antennae waving about, indicating the presence of a lobster. However, as soon as he got close or touched one of the antennae, it instantly withdrew out of reach. He had a hand spear with him, in the hope of somehow getting something to eat, but subconsciously carried it more as a form of assurance against… well, whatever he might need protection against.

This lobster situation seemed to require the use of such a tool, so he attacked the problem with vigor and cunning. After several attempts, he soon found that the techniques of hiding and the element of surprise—common to all hunting—were just as important here, too, and he soon had two medium lobsters snapping in the dinghy.

David spent several hours in the water over the next couple of days, diving the various reefs, trying his hand at spearing fish or lobster, or just plain cruising about, watching life on the streets of his new hometown.

On one particular reef, where the pattern of steep gullies and ridges predominated, there were a lot of caves near the sandy bottom, where he saw more large groupers than anywhere else, and he was determined to get one. He followed one after another down, to the limits of his breath, only to have it disappear under a ledge, either deeper than he could go or darker than he was willing to explore.

Once, while sneaking along the reef following a grouper, he was near the bottom, when he suddenly chanced upon a large, dark-gray form lying on the sand, just under the protective overhang of the reef. It was a shark, about six feet in length. David stared blankly at the form, slowly letting himself rise toward the surface. His mind rapidly placed it as a nurse shark, because of the finger-like barbels at its mouth, and the long, trailing tail. Knowing nurse sharks are not dangerous, he floated, relieved, the rest of the way to the surface.

Still watching where the shark was, he became aware of two other motionless forms below, partially hidden by the reef overhangs. *A popular place for the big guys,* he kidded himself, and turned to vacate the premises. But, as he turned to swim off, his way was blocked by a huge, gray form not fifteen feet from him.

How big that nurse shark was he didn't know. He could only stare as it slowly swam past, its long tail waving like a whip, in slow motion. Eyes wide, David tore through the water toward his dinghy, fin blades bent double with the thrust of his legs. He fairly rocketed up the side of the dinghy and fell into the protective center, panting with his effort and scare.

Once settled down, he began to chuckle at what must have been for the shark a very humorous sight: this strange human form tearing through the water like a steamboat, only to disappear in a small, gray mothership. *Now I know how visiting space aliens must feel, when confronting monstrous-looking humans.* He smiled even broader at the idea.

It was getting hotter and David was tired from the dive, so he began to pull in the dinghy anchor line. But it didn't come. It was caught. *Or else that shark has it in its mouth,* his mind leapt in panic. *Ridiculous,* he thought, and tugged harder. Nope, it was stuck. He rowed over the top of the anchor and pulled some more. *No go— it must be really hooked. Great!*

His mind raced to the complications and thoughts of the large shark increased.

Okay, let's handle this sensibly, like an adult, for Christ's sake. As he started to think, he put his hand to his head and ran his fingers slowly through his hair—much like his father did so often, when deep in thought. *It must be hooked on a piece of coral, or in a hole. So, I have to go down and pull it out.* Logical, but scary. The memory of the nurse shark was very fresh.

He stared at the water, as small waves slapped lightly against the dinghy like a snare drum, beating a slow tattoo. "Well, damn it, I've got to do something," he muttered with determination. And still he waited. But no one reached over to say, "That's okay, son, I'll take care of it." It was just him, all alone, standing up in this dinghy on a flat expanse of water, with a small, thin line of rope disappearing below, tying him to responsibility.

Slowly, he put his fins back on, then the mask and snorkel. He paused on the side of the dinghy and gently lowered himself in. The coral ridges and gullies leapt into view.

He rapidly wheeled about to get a 360° view. *No sharks anywhere.* And there went the anchor line, straight down to the side of a ridge where it hung, solidly snagged on some coral.

Without another thought, David snapped down and drove himself toward it. In an instant, he had lifted it free and left it to dangle in mid-blue, as he rose toward the welcoming gray dinghy.

In less than a minute the engine was purring, and he was eagerly headed toward *Endeavor*.

17

Shortly after he arrived at the islands, David found something in his roaming which was especially interesting, since it wasn't a part of the natural environment of the island world. On the other side of the little pod of islands from David's cove was a larger island, shaped like a large sickle—the blade forming a sweeping bay, open to the southeast; the handle a high, jumbled bluff, which pointed straight toward where *Endeavor* was anchored.

He had left this sickle-shaped island to explore last, because it was farthest from him and was also the most exposed; any foul weather that arose had easy access, over a large reef, to the beautiful beach which graced its eastern shore. Yet, despite this vulnerability, it seemed inexcusable to leave one island out of his explorations. So, one day, his dinghy at last ground to a halt on the gently sloping beach.

It was a fine beach, with powdery white sand stretching in a brilliant arc along the light-blue water, which gradually deepened and then became an undulating medley of colors, as it ran among the shallower and then deeper grassy areas of the bank.

At the high-tide line of the beach, small dunes had formed from the strong trade wind, and a small ridge of them ran up to a higher storm line, before the bushes and trees claimed the land. A few clumps of coconut palms were scattered along the mile of beach, but otherwise nothing remarkable was to be seen. Except for where the people had been.

Right where the gleaming sickle-blade beach joined the rocky handle was a place where there had been a fire. Of course, most of the remains had long been swept away by the tides, but enough of the evidence remained above the tide line to indicate that a fire had been lit—and a big one, too. Large, partially-burned logs lay half-buried in the sand, and the immediate vicinity was well-scavenged for fuel. Branches had been broken off small trees, and whole bushes were hacked off near the ground. Someone seemed to need a lot of wood to burn—an awful lot. *Why would they need such a big fire?* he wondered. With a fire like that on the wide-open beach, the light could be seen for miles across the east side of the bank.

David couldn't make sense of it, and so started on down the rest of the beach, hunting for shells along the tide line. About halfway to the end he came upon another fire area, not as large as the one at the handle, but still able to consume a lot of wood, as evidenced by the nearby hacked-up vegetation. The puzzle was getting more intriguing, and David was beginning to enjoy the mystery.

Now, if I find a big iron kettle and a big stake… And, his imagination was off again…

Twenty war canoes are being paddled furiously by painted heathens, as their quarry—a man and a woman clad in safari clothes (complete with pith helmets, of course)—run desperately in the soft sand, stumbling yet determinedly continuing. The canoes grate onto the beach and the feathered, spear-waving hordes erupt onto the beach. The man and woman look back. She screams. He tells her to get ahold of herself, and on they run.

The sound of the chanting is closer now, as the savages gain. Horrors! The woman falls and struggles to get up, her right hand outstretched pleadingly to the man. He hears her and looks back. What should he do? The masses are almost at her. To go back means certain death; to go on means a chance to live… but what kind of a life would that be, wondering for eternity if…

And the director yells, "Cut! They've got a problem with the chocolate pudding in the kettle."

In disgust at yet another costly delay, the dark-skinned man and woman throw down their helmets, as the white-skinned warriors toss their spears in disgust, and dive into the inviting water to wash off the sweat-smeared paint…

David was enjoying himself immensely.

He was finally almost to the end of the beach and was very hot, ready for a dip in the water himself, when another darkened area on the beach stopped him. There it was: another fire, just like the last one.

Now this is getting spooky, he thought, as his advertisement filming scenario reverted to its classic origins, and he looked suspiciously about. Nothing but birds in the trees and lizards scuttling about underneath. "Stupid," he muttered, and ran out into the water.

The cooling plunge felt great. From the water, he looked back at the beach. Just a nice beach, nothing else, and he slowly breast-stroked back in. Yet, what were the fires for? *Who the heck would go to all that trouble?*

The questions nagged at him as he walked back. The small tide was coming in now, almost to his beached dinghy, and it was getting late; he should be returning to the boat. Yet, he wanted to do one more thing before he left: the jumbled rocks of the handle were just too tempting to leave unclimbed. Besides, the height should provide a partial view of the entire bank and islands. Since he would eventually have to navigate that expanse so he could leave these islands, he figured his action was justified.

But it was no easy climb; the rocks were hot and sharp, and there wasn't a breath of air to be had, since he was in the lee of the trade wind. Within a few minutes, though, he was at an elevation high enough to get a good view, and he decided to stop. He picked a good spot, under a small tree which afforded some shade, and sat down in the breeze to reap his reward.

As expected, he could see out onto the bank, far enough to determine that sand bars and shallow places were amply abundant to make navigating the shallow sea a challenge.

Challenging, yes, but not impossible, he noted. He then turned toward the beach, arcing in beautiful proportion away from him.

Settling into his place more comfortably, his thoughts drifted to the fires, and he searched for where they should be, not sure that he could make out their location at this height and distance. But he was wrong; the ravages of the human activity on the vegetation were plain, since he knew what to look for.

He sat there, idly shifting his eyes from one spot to the other, noting the triangle that they would form if lines were drawn. Or a great big arc, unmistakable from even this height, let alone from an airplane…

And the humor of his pudding commercial soured, as he realized the significance of his discovery.

18

David lay gloomily on his bunk, feet propped against the bulkhead and arms crossed, staring at his feet. *Why here? Why not on some other island?* He had worked hard to get here; he deserved to be rewarded. *If they want to smuggle drugs, they could have at least picked someplace else for a drop, not my islands.* And now he'd have to leave sooner than expected.

He enjoyed being here, and had sharpened his boat-handling skills, but he still lacked the confidence he felt he needed, and he didn't like being pushed—he never had, not for anything. His mind rambled aimlessly in a mixture of self-pity, fear, and anger, but it produced nothing useful.

There wasn't anything he could do about it; the evidence was too clear. He had to admit that the island was a perfect place: easy to spot at night with the signal fires, drop the stuff, then put it on a stolen yacht, and head for the Bahamas and the States. These islands were off the usual yacht route, but not so far as to be suspicious, and still close enough to not waste a lot of fuel and time.

Of course, he could be wrong, but being honest with himself, there was no mistaking what had been going on here. He'd just have to get out. *No way I want to be caught by those guys.* The stories he heard circulating back in the Bahamas were just too real.

But, when? Who knew when they'd be back? Maybe tonight. Maybe a month from now. *Hell of a situation to be stuck in.* In frustration, he pushed himself off his bunk and climbed topside.

The sun was almost down, and with it the wind had abated,

bringing a stillness which allowed the bird calls on the islands to drift clearly across the water. This was a favorite time for David, when the glassy calmness of the water's surface delineated the eastern horizon into a sharp knife-edge of steely blue. He sat down in the cockpit and waited.

Shortly, as the sun neared the straight, dark line of the sea's horizon, it grew redder and larger, until it was almost twice its normal diameter. Then, the instant the sun touched the sea, the spectacle began and David smiled. He never tired of the sight. As that huge, glowing, yellow-reddish orb started to melt into the sea, a large pool began to form on the sea's surface, heap up and spread slightly, so that it soon took the shape of an old-fashioned mantle clock, or a dip of strawberry ice cream melting on the sidewalk. After that, the rest was quick; the base disappeared and the dome of the sun simply sank deeper and deeper, until... poof! It was gone. If he was lucky, there was an instant of green flash when the sun disappeared.

Darkness came fast then.

The glow of David's pleasure lasted a few minutes longer, until the coolness of the evening breeze rippled the water's surface... and the reality of modern-day pirates intruded brusquely.

David ended up spending the next morning diving on the reefs for fish and lobsters, since they had now become his primary food source, considering the almost empty food lockers. Afterward he was worn out, and quickly fell asleep on the deck, warming up and drying out. It had been a great time, and he relished the exhaustion he felt. Being rather tired, he couldn't concentrate on his problem very well, and relegated the task to the afternoon.

While munching away on a lunchtime snack, he took a look

around below--deck and decided that the pigpen in which he lived was a disgrace, so started picking things up. Shortly, his enthusiasm spread into his cabin and on to the rest of the boat, digging into corners and lockers which had not seen daylight for many days or weeks.

Finally finished, he stood proudly amid his handiwork, and was contented with the thought that his father would be very proud of his highly atypical efforts. The effort had been wearing, to be sure, so a decision about his problem was consigned yet farther into the future—to first thing the next morning, as soon as he arose.

But then, after sleeping in until almost noon that next day, David now decided that the supply of coconuts was low and needed replenishing. He was in the dinghy, ready to cast off for shore, when he suddenly stopped…

And finally quit running…

He had to face it; he had to lay plans. He was only deluding himself with all this busywork.

Dourly, he climbed back onto the boat and went down below. He now knew what he had to do.

Sitting at the chart table, David pulled out the chart which covered this area of the sea. It was a small-scale chart and didn't provide much detail, but it was all he had. At least it would help plot his route—its main purpose, anyway.

Puerto Rico lay maybe two days' sailing southeast, opposite from him across the Silverado Bank, depending on how well he did the sailing and navigating. He'd either have to go around the bank or across it. He hated to make the choice and stared grudgingly at the chart, letting his eyes and mind wander.

Suddenly, he stopped. There, at the far end of the bank, was a small dot with a name written beside it: "Esperanza Island".

An island! Down there!

He had been so intent on using the chart to find a way through the islands at this northern end, that he had neglected to look any further. It appeared to be very small. *Could be a mistake...* But, no—his islands here turned out to be as charted, so maybe this was, too.

Esperanza Island. Now that he had a goal he was elated, for he had been reluctant to head offshore again. He wasn't quite ready for that yet—later, but not just yet. And this... this small dot on the map he could reach by sailing the shallow sea of the bank. *Great!*

But, could I? He had only briefly looked at these shallow waters, with just that task in mind, and the chart before him wouldn't help at all, since detailed features were not indicated. It was probably much like the banks of the Bahamas: shifting sand bars and some rocky shoals, but basically very navigable once away from the fringing reef, he reassured himself.

But I'd feel better if I could examine it more carefully before setting out. So, why not take another look?

Since the sickle-shaped island he just visited had the highest point of land, he could see a long way from there, as his brief climb and look indicated, so that was where he needed to go. As he hurried to get into the dinghy and on his way, the string of decisions for preparation fell into place like dominoes.

It was now early afternoon and, if he hustled, he could get there before the water turned dark with shadows. The route he chose to climb was about the most brush-free he could find, but that also meant that the sun had full exposure to his sweating, toiling body, as he went up higher and higher.

Being on the west side, he knew he would see nothing of the bank to the south and east, and no wind could sufficiently reach its fingers around the hill to cool him off. In under an hour, however, he finally stood up in the refreshing breeze and gazed over the expanse of the bank.

Good plan!

The white and blue mottling of the sandy and grassy water reassured him of his decision. There were several long tentacles of sand bars reaching far into the distance, and a few brown bars of rock, but basically the rest was clear of obstacles. It was about forty miles directly to the island, and would be a good day's sail, considering that some detours would undoubtedly have to be taken.

Satisfied with what he had seen and resolved to set out the next day, he casually took one last, contemplative look at the islands he had come to claim.

And, as his gaze swept over the sickle-shaped island, he froze.

Almost hidden from sight, where the handle and blade of the island joined, was a large motor yacht, perhaps seventy to eighty feet long and very sleek—probably as fast as its Italian designer meant it to look. He was dumbfounded. He was too late; they were here. His mind went blank and he stood staring.

Finally realizing that he should at least get down off the silhouette of the hill, he moved back several feet, and sat partially hidden by a rock outcropping.

Very clever, he had to admit, since the yacht lay in a deep blue channel, which ran almost from the beach back around the handle, and wove through the islands, hidden from where *Endeavor* was anchored, until it terminated in a slight opening on the east side. The passage was well-concealed and would take someone with intimate knowledge of the islands to find. He had only stumbled on it by accident, during a diving trip.

So, that was how they got in? Then the drop must be tonight! They wouldn't hang around any longer than necessary, and take a chance of being discovered.

And, to add fire to David's problem, the only route through the bank went right by the yacht.

By the time he arrived back at his boat, however, David's frustration and fear had become tempered with curiosity. After all, there was a chance that they might not be smugglers, he tried unconvincingly to reason with himself. Regardless of whatever type of people were aboard the yacht, he decided he should find out what was going on, and when they might leave. He could easily approach from the opposite side of the island around dusk, and conceal himself in the undergrowth, close to the beach.

With a plan formed, he prepared to set out, since the sun was already low on the horizon.

It took a good bit of scrambling over rocks and through the brush—with small cuts and scrapes—to reach his destination, but he finally arrived. The sun was down by then, and shadows made it difficult to see very clearly, but he saw enough to convince him of his initial conclusion.

The large fire area near the yacht was already heaped with cut brush, apparently hacked off by the sinister-looking machetes stuck upright nearby in the sand. He wriggled himself along the ground, until he was able to slide into a depression among the dunes.

The great, white yacht sat silently at anchor, like a large toy in a bathtub, looking rather out-of-place in the small bay of still water. Deck lights were on, as well as some in the cabins, and these gave the boat an incongruously festive air.

Voices were coming from down the beach, and David scrunched even closer to the ground. It was nearly dark, but he could still make out five people: four men and one woman. They spoke Spanish, so he was unable to understand the conversation, but it was fairly clear that some of them were unhappy about something. Most of the men were Latinos, dressed in work pants or shorts, but one was apparently American, from his occasional mixed English and Spanish contributions to the ongoing discussion.

The men were mostly young but the woman was older—in her late thirties, perhaps. But David wasn't good at guessing ages. She was Latino as well, and was dressed in dark slacks and a loose, striped blouse. She gestured sharply to the men when addressing them, and David could see that not everything she said was agreeable to them. They lit a small fire near the brush pile, and sat or stood around as though waiting for something, it seemed to David.

Suddenly, a commotion on the yacht diverted everyone's attention, especially David's. The slender figure of a girl in a white dress erupted from one of the cabin doors and ran along the deck passageway, aft to the sundeck.

Immediately behind her came a well-dressed young man, shouting at her as he ran to catch her. But she was quick of foot and sidestepped his grab at her arm, as she pushed a lounge chair into his path.

At last they came to a stand-off, each on opposite sides of a table, yelling at each other. The anger of the girl was unmistakable, even though David couldn't understand her. The man tried to advance toward her again and she pushed the table, causing him to yell loudly and gesture wildly. The group about the fire seemed to be enjoying the action very much, and jostled each other as they talked.

The woman finally called out in a severe voice to the arguing couple, and in two short sentences managed to bring their remaining discussion down to a less audible volume. The five then returned to the fire.

The young man and girl argued for a few minutes more, before she wheeled about and stalked back down the corridor, disappearing into a doorway. The young man raised his arms in supplication, shrugged his shoulders, and turned in the opposite direction.

It was quite dark now, and the small fire more clearly lit the faces and forms of the men and woman sitting around its perimeter. It was only at this point that David noticed some of the group were armed, when the firelight glinted off the polished mechanism of a rifle or pistol.

It might be a long night, David began to think, and he settled more comfortably, then rather complacently waited for the action to unfold. His eyes drooped more sleepily the longer he lay there…

19

Someone was shouting in the distance, *perhaps from the yacht. It was unclear to David what was being said, though he had the feeling it was something about an airplane.*

An airplane! This was it!

David struggled to tune his sleepy brain to the flurry of activity which now burst forth. The group on the beach quickly rose and moved toward the yacht's two waiting launches, except for the American, who stayed behind. The boats were soon headed off just along the beach, and their motors eventfully died in the distant darkness, as their destinations were reached.

A fair breeze had picked up and replaced the silence, with the swishing sound of waves lapping on the beach, and the rustling of branches in the trees and bushes. The American had gone off somewhere out of sight, and had not returned.

Then David noticed a figure clambering over the side of the yacht, into a small inflatable, and starting for shore, out of reach of the bright pool of luminescence from the ship's lights. David's attention increased, and he intently followed the dinghy as it landed on the shore, just down from the fire. After about two minutes, a slight figure appeared at the edge of the fire. It was the girl from the yacht—he was positive of it, and his interest perked up considerably.

She seemed to be looking for something on the ground, or at least near the fire. But it was also apparent that she was afraid of being discovered, since she nervously kept glancing in the direction of the other fires. What was she doing, he wondered? Then he knew: she had found a pistol. She tucked it into her waistband and crept off into the bush.

"What the hell?" he muttered aloud. But the more he thought about it,

the clearer it became. She wasn't a part of them. She was a captive—perhaps the last survivor of the yacht's crew or even the daughter of the murdered owners. That must be it. What other explanation could there be?

A rising moon enabled David to follow her movements for a distance, and he could see her coming right toward him. What now?

Well, he would make his presence known, explain who he was, and help her escape. Yes, that was a sensible plan. After all, she was beautiful and in need of help, and he was seventeen and nearly an adult… Thoughts of an affectionate reward flooded his eager mind.

She nearly stumbled upon him, before he rose and called to her, "Wait! I'm a friend."

Startled, the girl uttered a small cry, before pulling her gun and asking in a frightened voice, "Wh-who are you?" There was a strong Spanish accent.

"Shh, I'm a friend. I'm not with those guys. I've got my own boat nearby, and just stumbled on all this."

She kept the gun in front of her, but he could tell she was beginning to relax.

"Look, I don't know how you got in with these people, but I'll help you get away."

Silence. He took a chance. "Were your parents killed when those people hijacked your boat?"

The gun lowered, and the girl began to cry softly. "Yes, they were." She struggled with the emotion and tears. "And they are keeping me… for their pleasure, after they transfer the cocaine." She broke down crying.

David rushed forward and caught her as she collapsed. They fell to their knees on the sand, where David pulled her to his shoulder, held her tight, and stroked her long, dark hair. She wept freely.

"It's okay now," he comforted her. "We'll get out of here. Shh, not so loud. Someone might hear."

A voice just behind them broke in, "Hey. Who's out there?" It was the American. But he hadn't spotted them yet.

Instantly, David leapt at the man as he turned, looking for the source of the voices. David grasped the man's rifle and pulled it tight up against his throat. The American was heavier than David, but David clung to the man's back, with the rifle pulled tight like a vise. Gasping for air, the man twisted and turned to get the thing off his back, but he was growing weaker and finally collapsed. David pulled the rifle out of the man's grip and stood proudly over his conquest.

The girl was up by now and threw herself at David, pulling his head down and firmly placing her full, sweet lips against his. She pressed her body warmly to his and held on tight, for what seemed like forever. "Oh, thank you, thank you!" she effused, as she placed her head against his chest. "Let's go away from this awful place," she added, pleading.

But David was firm. "There's something we have to do first," he said, resolutely: "we've got to stop them from following us. We've got to blow up your yacht."

The girl gasped.

"I know you hate to do it as much as I do, but we've got to save ourselves… and avenge the death of your parents."

The girl nodded, and they set off to the dinghy.

They went to work quickly, and in a brief time were aboard the yacht, and had rigged the fuel tanks to detonate as soon as David and the girl were off the boat and ashore.

Already the drone of an airplane could be heard above, and the fires down the beach were flaming. But the first signal fire near the yacht was still unlit; it wouldn't be long before someone realized something was wrong and returned. David and the girl had to move quickly.

Just as they were coming up from the engine room and stepping on deck, they nearly bumped into the young man with whom the girl had earlier argued. Surprised, he asked something in Spanish, then realized David wasn't one of the crew.

He started to shout, but David dove at him, and the two of them tumbled to the deck. The man was a good fighter, and he stunned David with several blows, but David fought back however he could, kicking the man in the groin, doubling him up with pain. David then quickly shoved him against the metal cabin side; there was a dull thud as the man's head bounced, and the body slumped to the deck.

"Quick! We've got to go." David reached for the girl's hand and they *ran to the boarding ladder.*

The other signal fires were blazing brightly now, and the plane was circling above. But another motor was also getting louder: one of the launches was returning, at full speed.

They jumped into the dinghy and David pulled at the oars, straining as never before. The ship could blow at any minute, and the launch was almost upon them! Suddenly, the girl stood up.

"What are you doing?" David asked incredulously. She glanced at him, her eyes flashing in the wavering ship's light, and her hair flowing in the breeze, framing the beauty of her face.

"I forgot something. I've got to go back."

"You're crazy!" David cried. "The ship's going to blow up!"

"I'll meet you on the beach." She dove into the dark water and began to swim.

David dropped the oars and scrambled to the front of the dinghy. "Wait! I don't even know your name!" he called out.

The girl broke her stroke and turned back to face him. There was a coy smile upon her face now, somehow very familiar to David. The gentle waves rolled the surface, lifting David and the girl slowly up and down, the dark, purplish color of the waves reflecting golden splashes of light from the ship. As she slowly started to swim on her back, she grinned impishly and said, "My name is—"

The exploding ship behind her drowned the words. Flames engulfed her form and boiled toward David, as he fell onto the floor of the dinghy, and covered his head against the searing heat and roaring sound…

…David jerked his head up from the sand, in a sudden start from his dream. A very bright fire was burning quite close by, and the distant drone of engines suddenly roared overhead. Confusion reigned for a moment, but then a glance at the yacht—floating as before, with lights burning brightly—and the signal fires down the beach put everything into perspective. He rubbed his eyes to clear his sleepy vision.

The fire was so big that he could feel the heat, even from where he was. All about him the ground was illuminated, except in the slight depression behind the dune, where he was hiding. There was no escape now; he had to stay put.

The plane roared by on a final pass, and a string of floating lights, twinkling like Christmas candles in a midnight mass, were left behind on the water. As the plane noise was rapidly swallowed by the darkness, the motors of the launches came to life as they did their work. Soon, the lit floating bundles of cocaine were all snagged aboard the launches, and they started for the yacht.

"So that's how they do it…" David muttered. *Pretty neat. No currents, no underwater hazards, nothing to get in their way—except me. And I'm not about to get myself killed,* he reassured himself, the precariousness of his situation impressing on him.

However, this logic somehow seemed to contradict something within him very strongly, like some very strong emotional experience he had recently felt. It seemed to be something about the fuzzy dream, which was rapidly fading, but he couldn't clearly focus on it.

Besides, a new distraction appeared. Three figures now assembled on the sun deck of the yacht: a younger man, a gray-haired older man, and… the young girl. *Yes, like in my dream!* David's emotions quickened, and a warmth arose in him as he stared at her. He seemed almost able to feel the softness of her body pressed against his, and the taste of the full lips which graced her beautiful face. The sensation was familiar, yet mystifying.

But the mood was abruptly shattered when the older man, in response to a call he received on a handheld radio, relayed a message to the other two, and they broke out in a cheer and hugged each other. A champagne cork popped off into the darkness and glasses tinkled, as the three made a toast to their success.

Feeling both confused and disgusted, David slowly lowered himself to the sandy ground and grimly began to wait out the still-blazing fire. The fire had been well supplied with wood, and continued burning on into the night.

David drifted in and out of sleep, as he kept assessing the fire's condition and his opportunity to escape.

The coals finally cooled and shed no more light. It wasn't until three o'clock in the morning that he finally tumbled into his bunk.

20

David was very tired the next day, and slept in late. He suspected that the smugglers would have left early in the morning, and when he got around to cautiously checking later in the day, he found that he was correct; only fresh ashes remained at the fire stations. The beach was as serene and perfect as before, oblivious to the role it played in the lives of thousands of people farther north, in the mainland of the U.S. Since the cocaine runners were gone, there was now no big rush for David to leave.

However, he had made a decision and was determined to stick with it. Besides, this paradise of his for the past several days had begun to fade in its attraction, somehow tainted by the events of the previous night. He was also looking forward to finding out more about his dad, of course. But tomorrow would be soon enough, he concluded. Much of the preparation had already been done during his cleaning spree, and he needed a decent morning start, anyway. So, the remainder of the day was spent tending to necessary details.

The day of departure rose with a clear sky and a steady but light north-easterly trade wind. David ate a quick breakfast and pulled anchor.

The sun rising in the east was often in his eyes, and made it difficult to see the seafloor as well as he wanted, but, as it rose, it got easier to figure out the shallow and deep areas.

He motored for the first half-hour, wending his way along sand bars and flats, until he reached what seemed to be the deeper water which extended toward his goal, if his memory of the view from the hill served him correctly. Sails were raised and, with the motor off, the old sounds of the water and the boat returned to keep him company.

David was surprised that it felt good to be off and traveling again. Good to feel the rhythm of progress. Good just to have a goal again! For the first time, he consciously realized that this must be something of how his father felt about sailing; what it was like to have some type of goal he could actively work toward, and see his progress every second of the going.

Furthermore, David was able to enjoy this knowing that it was his direct efforts which made it possible; his skill in contention with the wiles of nature, playing upon the mechanics of a peculiar human invention: a sailboat. Small bits of further memories of his dad peeped at David and, finding the dragon of recent anguish asleep, stayed to keep him company.

The small group of islands diminished in size behind him, and gradually had their bottoms melted off, as the Earth's curvature on the distant sea will do. Soon they were completely gone, and he was surrounded by nothing but water again.

Yet, this time there was a difference: all he had to do was look over the side and there the bottom was, nine or ten feet down. And it went on like that for mile after mile, hour after hour, changing depth by maybe a foot or two, but otherwise flat—very flat. At times, when the wind slackened and the surface was less ruffled, David could see the bottom quite clearly and would stand at the bow for long periods, catching passing glimpses of conch shells, amber-colored starfish, and the innumerable cone-shaped mounds of worms, which transformed the white, sandy bottom into a panorama of prehistoric volcanism. Occasionally, the boat's shadow would spook a ray, and it would glide rapidly off, wings rippling. Once, David even startled a fairly good-sized nurse shark, and he wondered what it found of interest way out there. But, except for a few birds, the passage was rather devoid of action—which he was very happy for.

It was getting late in the afternoon, and David had yet to sight any land. He had to admit that the target he was trying to hit was quite small, so he kept checking and rechecking his dead-reckoning line and GPS position. While at the island cove, he had done some more reading on navigation and felt a lot better about what he was doing now. But this new landfall eluded him, and he began to worry.

When there was about an hour left before sunset, he spotted an object on the horizon—not quite where it was supposed to be, but at least it was something he could see. In another twenty minutes, it showed sufficiently above the horizon to definitely be an island. He scanned the surrounding circle of flat, dark water and, without any sign of others around, David concluded that it had to be Esperanza.

But how did I end up so far off? This fact bothered him, until at last he remembered a plausible explanation, one that his father had concluded several times during their cruising the Bahamas: a tidal current; there must have been a current. It seemed hard to believe that even out on this immense ocean-lake anything could affect the water, but it would make sense. All that water had to move in some direction, with the tidal pull of the moon. He felt better now, knowing that the source of error was not entirely due to some inherent ineptitude of his as a seaman, but only from his lack of experience as a navigator. With the mystery solved, he changed course and continued.

It was shortly afterward that he hit the first sand bar. The sudden bumping and lurching of the boat severely shook David, and he leapt to the deck to see what had happened. A huge white expanse stretched before him. Immediately, he jumped back into the cockpit and spun the wheel. The boat did not turn much at first, but as the wind filled the sails on the other tack, it heeled over and the keel lifted free of the sand. Now he was headed more or less away from the island.

Oh, great! Now what? He questioned. With the rapidly gathering dusk, it was getting very difficult for him to see the bottom any distance ahead. The bar seemed to trend toward the southeast, but he wasn't sure; it was just too dark. He'd have to stop where he was, before he got into worse trouble. Since the day's wind had been steady, and no cloud banks loomed on the horizon, he figured it would be safe to stay there.

With the sails finally dropped and the anchor securely embedded in the sandy bottom, David's world seemed to come to a standstill once again, with blank expanses of water and sky surrounding, the wind waning until even the rigging no longer sang, and him sitting alone, without knowledge of the existence of the rest of humanity.

But it truly didn't matter how distorted his perception of reality might now be; he was almost there, and he was tired. In the morning, he would be able to see where to go. There would be plenty of time from now on—that was what mattered most.

The sun melted into the sea, and on the opposite side the darkness of the east drew overhead, like a translucent window shade. Venus appeared in the west, an unblinking eye, and a quarter-moon materialized to eventually cast a milky light on the shallow sea, upon which he and the boat floated.

David ate a simple meal and watched the transformations of his universe, until darkness revealed the light of billions of years ago, and then he went to bed.

Early morning found David up the mast, standing on the lower spreader, to get a higher viewpoint of where he needed to go. The small difference in elevation made a great difference in his line of sight; he could now see that he had to head southwest a mile or so, turn to the southeast and follow a dark, grassy channel, which appeared to eventually lead to the island.

Encouraged by what he had found, he climbed carefully back down to the cabin top, started the engine, and set about weighing anchor. Finding his way to the grassy channel wasn't as easy now that he was again at surface level, where sight was restricted, and everything lay hidden until one was almost upon it. But, after a half-hour of mistakes and corrections, he seemed to be on the right track, and was soon rapidly approaching his goal.

The island was indeed quite small—maybe four or five miles in the longest direction—and seemed to be shaped like an irregular piece of cheese, out of which numerous bites had been taken. In fact, the bites were small coves which had beautiful little beaches lining their shores, in between rocky headlands ruggedly eroded by waves.

Typically, the land was heavily vegetated, like those of his prior landfall. But, unlike those islands, there were no high cliffs or hills; small rises on the headlands seemed to suffice here. Neither was there a close fringing reef on the side from which he approached. But in the distance to the north and east, he could make out what appeared to be breakers tumbling in profusion. Regardless, Esperanza did not seem to be as boxed in as the other islands, and he was thankful for that.

In a short time, he was standing on the bow of *Endeavor*, staring at the anchor chain as it stretched in a gentle arc from the bow into the water, and onto the white sand bottom. Since no wind penetrated to ripple the surface in the small cove, it again seemed as though the boat was suspended in the air by this thin line of metal links.

Ashore he could hear mockingbirds singing from the trees, and the gentle swishing sound of small waves collapsing on the beach. The sun was almost overhead and he had the whole day ahead of him.

Dad would have liked this place. The thought brought on a smile.

All the next day David explored the island, checking out each beach and cove he came across. All were quite similar and picturesque; dropping anchor in any of them would be equally satisfying.

There was one very small cove which was sort of neat, though kind of secret, since the entrance wasn't open but restricted, until it became broader inside—big enough for one boat to swing on its anchor. Other than that, it had no special charm, but the secretiveness made it especially appealing to David, and he resolved to move there in a day or so.

To his relief, he also found evidence of other visitors. Not the smuggler type, but good old roasting-a-hotdog-around-the-fire type folk. *Probably yachtsmen, like me,* he decided, from the size and shape of the firepits.

A few bottles and cans had been left by careless visitors, and he collected these and took them aboard, to join his own small bag of waste items. Given this evidence of how much the island was visited, David finally concluded that he might indeed—as he had hoped—sight another boat, and he frequently turned an eye seaward to the horizon.

On the second day, he was lounging in the cockpit after lunch, scanning over the island—watching the sandpipers and other small shorebirds in their nervous little pecking dance, as they followed the waves on the beach—when he noticed a tall pole above the treetops, which he hadn't seen before. Actually, there were two, one shorter than the other.

Strange I didn't see them before, the thought muddled about in his half-awake mind. And, just as he at last made out the lines coming from their tops, it dawned on him that they were masts.

Another boat!

A tall and a short one made it a ketch, and a fairly good-sized one. Why hadn't he seen it before? *Of course, stupid—it must have just come in this morning,* he chastised himself.

His jumbled thoughts leapt to all sorts of absurdities, before he managed to whip them into shape. Highly unlikely they were smugglers, with a cruising boat like that—probably—and he shelved that likelihood.

So, they must be boat people. His mind then ran with the possibilities that entailed: where they were from, how many, were they friendly or stuck-up, and on and on.

It all ground to a halt, though, after he had progressed in his imaginary meeting to the point of when the questions regarding him would begin. His mind went blank. After all, what was he supposed to say?

"Oh, my dad fell overboard a week ago, and I was asleep and didn't know how to run the boat, so he just floated away… but somebody found and saved him," he mocked himself.

David shoved his hands hard into the pockets of his shorts and clenched his fists. "Shit! What a fraud I am!" he cursed aloud, wishing harder than ever that he could just go back to that horrible night and wake up when his dad had shaken him. *If I had just woken up!*

He struggled again and again to revive that hazy moment, but he failed. No amount of wishing could make it turn into reality. He couldn't go back; he had to go on. His father used to remind David, again and again, when he would want to quit—be it swimming lessons, the basketball team he tried to make, or the math assignments he hated—that he just had to keep plugging onward. He'd say, "You can't do anything about what is past; it's the future that you can change. Always remember that and don't give up."

In his mind's eye, he conjured up scene after scene when his dad spewed different versions of that concept, as David stood in the midst of his failed efforts. He hated it when his dad gave that little speech. It was always the same idea, and sounded so pious and goody-goody. But even then he knew it was true, and more so now.

So, David pulled in the reins and calmed down.

21

The yacht was ketch-rigged alright, and 45-50 feet long. With its multiple masts and sails, long, graceful bowsprit, center cockpit, and multi-level deck arrangement, the boat made *Endeavor* seem like a simple toy. *I'd hate to have to sail that one by myself,* David mused, as he rowed around the headland in his dinghy.

At first, he couldn't see anyone on deck or in the cockpit. He checked for a dinghy and, not spotting one, looked toward the beach that he could now see clearly. There it was, drawn up to the high-water mark—and there were people; four figures slowly walked back toward the dinghy, checking for shells. He adjusted his oar stroke and headed for them.

After landing, it took him a couple of minutes to stroll on down to where the strangers were. He was hesitant to approach them, but at the same time was drawn by the need within. It was a family with two girls, David noted happily—one around twelve years old and the other about his age, or a little older.

The younger one drew the other's attention to David's form walking toward them, and they shared a few words. The man and woman both wore broad-rimmed hats, so David couldn't see their faces too well. Everyone was intent on shell-collecting, but they had surely seen him rowing and knew he was there. Still, he decided he'd better call out a greeting first, since he was the one who came to their beach. When just within easy hailing distance, David called out:

"Hi, there. I saw your boat and thought I'd come to say hello.

It's been a while since I've seen anyone," he felt obligated to add.

The man and woman looked up, gave a short wave, and the woman answered back, "Hi. Nice beach, isn't it?"

"Yeah, it sure is," he responded, as he kept walking on toward them. "Find anything interesting?"

"Oh, a few odds and ends. Carrie found a very nice bonnet shell. Show him, Carrie," the mother turned and urged the younger girl. They met and David looked at the three-inch bonnet, perfectly shaped with its curling lip, and tan and white checks.

"Nice," he smiled and handed it back. Carrie's round, freckled face beamed, and she put it back in her collecting bag.

"So, how long have you been here?" the man asked, as they all started to walk back toward the dinghies.

Instantly suspicious, David glanced over. The man was quite a bit taller than David's father and more heavily built. He had a short, graying beard which jutted out from his chin and, with the straw hat pulled down to protect his eyes, made him seem rather stern. But there was no indication of this in his voice.

"Two days now. I just got here."

The man glanced inquisitively over at David, so he added, "My boat's over there, in the next cove." David motioned to where the very topmost tip of *Endeavor*'s mast could be seen above the trees.

No one spoke for a couple of steps, but it was obvious that the woman was curious about something. David tried to take an interest in the bare beach beneath his feet. "Sounds like you're alone. Are your parents aboard?"

He looked quickly at her, a rather plain but handsome woman, with her dark brown hair pulled back to a knot at the nape of her neck. Her eyes showed open acceptance, but the slightly raised right eyebrow gave away the intent of her curiosity.

"No. No, they aren't right now," David stumbled, as he cursed his lack of a well thought out plan. "They're back at home in the States—Pennsylvania," he added. Everyone shot a glance at him. He'd have to come up with some kind of an explanation.

"I'm out on my own," he added the obvious. "They couldn't come right now, so I'm taking the boat… on to the Virgin Islands," he finally completed the thought. "They'll meet me there."

"That's a pretty long trip to do single-handed, for a young fella like yourself," the husband commented. "You got a pretty good boat, I take it?" He was obviously either suspicious of the truth of the story, or doubtful of the sanity of David's parents.

"Oh, yeah," David quickly put in, "I've got a good boat— thirty-six feet and well built." His reply didn't faze the man's expression.

"I think it's pretty neat," a voice interjected from behind, and David turned. It was the older girl. "Not many parents would trust their kids to do something like that." She emphasized the word "trust".

The man broke into a laugh and turned to his daughter. "What's the matter? Don't you think we'd let you take *Dawn Treader* out by yourself?" he teased. The whole family seemed to be amused by the idea of the girl handling the big ketch by herself, and shared the joke.

"Daddy!" she scolded him as she smiled. "I just meant…"

"I know what you meant," he raised a fending hand. "And, if we had a smaller boat, I'd probably let you do the same thing. You're a pretty good sailor." He shot her a wink.

They were suddenly at the dinghies. "I guess we should introduce ourselves," the woman announced and smiled. "I'm Colleen; this is my husband, Dennis; our youngest daughter, Carrie; and this is Cindy." She pulled Cindy with a tug at the waist, and they both grinned. "We kept all our women's names in the Cs."

"Well, I'm David. I guess the men have at least two Ds," he added awkwardly, trying to lighten things, and it seemed to work;

Dennis and Colleen gave him a firm handshake to finish the ritual. Carrie's was a quick half-shake and Cindy's was warm.

He hadn't yet found an excuse to look Cindy full in the face, and did so now. Like her mother and the rest of the family, Cindy wasn't outstandingly good-looking, but attractive. Her cheeks and nose were nicely rounded and, together with her quick brown eyes, they gave her a somewhat intent look—not worried, but very attentive to what was happening around her. David got the feeling that she didn't miss a thing, and that made him somewhat apprehensive.

But, at the same time, she had an openness conveyed in her manner, which set him at ease. She seemed to confront everything fully and frontally, like the handshake that left David's hand still tingling. He wasn't used to such forwardness and, in half-embarrassment, turned aside. He could still feel her eyes, though.

"Okay," Colleen laughed, "now that we know who's who, how about coming aboard for something to eat? It's almost lunchtime."

"Yeah, I'm hungry!" Carrie agreed, as she threw her bag into the dinghy.

"Sure, I guess so," David decided, and grinned. He was dying to escape his usual boring basics and eat someone else's food.

"We'll see you at the boat, then," Dennis added, and began pulling their inflatable toward the water. Cindy gave David a hand with his boat, and the two dinghies headed toward *Dawn Treader*.

Lunch was just a large sandwich, fresh fruit, and lemonade, but with fresh lettuce, tomatoes, and Swiss cheese, it made his peanut butter, jelly, and crackers seem like prison fare. It was great to be able to talk to other people, too—he never thought he'd admit that. Truthfully, it seemed like he was doing lots of talking, as he related his recent adventures with the smugglers and exploring the islands across the bank.

In short order, he had managed to fabricate a sensible sequence of events, which covered the time from when he and his father had left Florida to the present. The only thing he had to do was leave his dad out of the picture and just proceed with the rest intact. He felt it was quite clever, though there was a nagging ache about excluding his dad. But why get into all that? What purpose would it have way out here?

He had already decided to make contact with home when he reached Puerto Rico, to see how his dad was doing—and what he was to do next, as well. He felt he didn't need to drag his shame out to display before strangers. This was a deed best done in the private confines of a telephone booth, somewhere out there in a distant port, when he could explain what happened.

The family, it turned out, was from Connecticut, and had been cruising aboard their ketch for about six months, taking a sabbatical leave to see how they liked it. Dennis and Colleen were both within about two years of retirement and, if the experiment proved successful, they would sell the house ashore and live permanently aboard. So far it seemed to have suited everyone.

The girls both voiced some occasional dissatisfaction with the fragmentary relationships they had to rely on, with other boat kids their age, but it also provided a steady stream of new faces to meet. They both appeared ready to accept this situation—for a little while longer, anyway.

At mid-afternoon, David thanked them and excused himself, saying that he had some things to do on the boat. The food and conversation had been great, but he was getting a little tired of the adult conversation level he was obligated to maintain. If his dad had been there, David could have sat back much as Carrie and Cindy did, and just add bits of information now and then, rather than being right up there tossing it back and forth all the time. That's the sort of interaction he was used to, and he missed it. The thought did once cross David's mind that maybe his dad didn't like having to play the role all the time, either, just as David found he didn't.

More importantly, though, David hadn't had a chance at all to talk with Cindy by herself, and he greatly wanted to do that. Just before he cast off in his dinghy, while Cindy was on deck untying the painter for him, he took the opportunity to suggest, in a lowered voice, "Maybe I could come by tomorrow morning, and we could go to the beach or something?"

"Sure. That'd be fun. I'll make us a lunch to take along, too. Okay?" She wore that tight little smile and sort of intent look in her eyes, which David had noticed at times during the afternoon. It was puzzling to him exactly what it meant. It was as though she had some secret she was bursting to tell, or a surprise to spring. He couldn't resolve the mystery, but the look was burned in his mind, and would torment him all the rest of the day and night.

"Sounds great," he grinned. "Well, so long," he awkwardly added, and she dropped the line into his boat. It sounded rather ridiculous to say that, since he was just going around the corner, but… *What the hell—who cares?* He waved to her as he pulled away and headed toward *Endeavor*.

Of course, he had absolutely nothing essential to get back to the boat for, and he just stood in the cockpit for several minutes, looking at the mast tops of the ketch showing above the island. He wondered what she was doing right then and tried several possibilities, enjoying the images which once more let him be with her. More importantly, what did she think of him? For this question, he was unable to come up with anything remotely definitive.

He sat down and stared at the horizon. *She seemed to like me okay. That is, she didn't barf or anything when she saw me.* And he smiled. *But seriously, what did she do or say to let me know?* He tried to run back over the visit in detail. He came up with a blank. A lot of the time she had sat sort of behind him, off to one side. He caught her looking at him a couple of times, but the look didn't show anything; it was just that open, intent gaze of hers—the kind which made you want to ask something, to learn what made that person tick. She had talked freely enough—as much as a kid usually does in that situation with parents around—and she had a wonderful full laugh and smile. David liked that, since he was a bit hesitant to do either one.

He finally concluded that he couldn't come up with anything—except that she picked up on his suggestion for tomorrow quite quickly, so maybe…

He broke off his gaze of the horizon. He would go nuts if he didn't quit guessing. He stood up, stripped off his shorts in one jerk, and did a looping dive over the lifeline and into the water. The water was a shock for a second and broke the train of thought.

He swam hard for a ways and then, winded, turned about to tread water and look back at the small boat, floating peacefully, ignorantly in the cove. Just like on picture postcards, he thought amusedly, and slowly breast-stroked back.

22

The next morning, David was up early and eager to go see Cindy, but 7:00 a.m. was a little too soon. He spent the next two hours dawdling around the boat, picking up this and that to move from one spot to the next, and then back again to its original location.

Frustrated with housecleaning, he finally went topside and just watched the gulls and terns wheeling about over the water's surface, hunting for food. Nearing nine o'clock he figured he had waited a decent-enough time, jumped in the dinghy, and set off.

"Hi!" David called out to Dennis and Colleen, who were sitting in the cockpit finishing some coffee when he reached the ketch.

"Morning. Looks like another beautiful day," Colleen smiled. She always seemed to be such a cheerful person. A little too much to be believable, David mused, but maybe she was just always happy, as impossible as it sounded. "Cindy," she called below, "David's here."

"I know," came a voice from below.

"Have a seat," Dennis offered, and pushed some gear out of the way.

"Thanks." David struggled to think up some adult small-talk, but couldn't think of anything to break the seemingly awkward silence. However, Colleen and Dennis apparently didn't mind the lack of conversation, and simply drank their coffee and watched the sea life around them.

"Where was it you said you went to school?"

Startled by the voice, David jumped slightly. "What? Oh, I went to McCaskey High. It's over on the east side of Lancaster," he responded to Colleen's question. "It's not a great big school," he added, glad to have some conversation again, "so it's an okay place, I guess."

Cindy appeared from below to save him. Although she wore just a pair of tan shorts and a simple pullover shirt, she still looked great to David, all fresh and radiant. She gave him a quick "Hi" and a smile, then asked her mother where the small cooler was for their lunch. She disappeared below for a minute and then returned. "Ready?"

"Sure."

"Where're you going to be and when'll you be back?" her father asked.

Cindy glanced at David. "We're just going to the beach here, right?"

"Uh, sure. Maybe hike around a little. There's a path over at that end," he motioned, "that leads along the top of the headland and to the next beach. We might take that for a while."

"We'll be back early afternoon," Cindy added. "Anyway, we'll be right close, so you can yell or send Carrie out in the dinghy. We won't get lost," she added, in a reassuring jest.

"Okay. Have fun," her mother smiled, as they started to leave.

David climbed in the dinghy first and took the cooler Cindy handed down to him. Then she got in, too, scooted back toward David to balance the boat, and smiled that tight smile of hers, as she moved closer to him. Her eyes twinkled in the bright sun. David happily pulled hard at the oars.

At the beach, they found a tree which would provide shade for the cooler and stashed it there. Both David and Cindy were feeling somewhat self-conscious, so they simply started walking up the beach, in the direction of the northeast headland.

They didn't talk for a while, just kicked at the sand as they walked, and stooped to pick up tiny shells from the tide line. For once, David didn't mind the silence; it was just good enough to be with her. Cindy didn't seem to mind, either; she appeared to be simply enjoying the walk and being out in the sun. Eventually, they began a patter of small-talk on a variety of topics, and soon reached the end of the beach.

"Want to go out on the point? There's sort of a trail up there I found yesterday." David motioned to the rocky rise above them.

"Okay. Lead the way."

"Watch out for the sharp rocks. Some of them can slip under your sandals," he cautioned.

In a mock frown, she replied, "I'm not exactly helpless, you know. I've been around a bit, after all."

"I didn't mean…" David started to explain.

"I know what you meant, silly," she grinned. "Get your butt in gear, or we'll never get there."

David gave a salute, "Yes, ma'am!" and started off at a good clip.

Even though the point of land jutting out between the two coves wasn't very high, it was a nice place at which to sit and look out. A gently arcing beach graced each small bay, and in the southern one *Dawn Treader* floated—a jewel in a small pool of glass.

Farther south, in the indentation which marked the cove where *Endeavor* was, it was just possible to see the sloop sitting quietly like the ketch, but much smaller.

"What's the name of your boat?" They had both been looking in that direction.

"*Endeavor.*"

"Who named it?" she turned toward David.

"I guess my dad did. I never thought about it."

"Well, what's it supposed to mean? I mean, why did he call it that?"

David pursed his lips as he thought. "I guess I don't know."

Then he added, after a moment's pondering, "Maybe it's because he was so persistent about things. He wasn't what you would call particular about everything; he just, well, stuck with what he was doing." David chuckled. "He was always after me about finishing what I started and not giving up. Always *'Stick with it, stick with it'.* I used to hate to have him say that."

"And, now?"

He didn't say anything for a couple of seconds. "I guess I wouldn't mind it now. I've sort of gotten better about that lately." Excruciating recent memories came to mind.

"David?"

He turned toward her.

"You talk about your father as if he was in the past," she began gently. "Did I miss something back there, when we met yesterday? I thought he and your mother were coming to meet you?"

His heart missed a beat and he glanced quickly at her. "No, he's not. I mean, of course he's alive. It was just the way I said it." David tried not to sound confused. "You asked about the name and the name brought up the past; I just got it said wrong." His voice had an edge of sharpness.

"I didn't mean anything. I'm sorry."

She did look sorry, and he didn't want things to get started off wrong, so he added, "No big deal. Okay?" She smiled and then looked off sort of behind them, to the north.

"What's over that way?"

David sought her direction. "Oh, more of the same. Over closer to the reefs, the coves get more wave action, so sometimes some nice breakers reach them and they're fun to play in. Some good diving, too. Do you skin-dive?" he asked, as the possibility of further activities together seemed to be expanding.

"Of course," she teased. "I'd be crazy if I didn't, being on a boat. It's great!"

Encouraged, David told about some of his experiences, and

found she had felt similarly when she started diving. He even
began to tell about the big nurse shark, and was going to alter the
story slightly, but at the last minute decided to tell it straight, and
admit his fear during the incident. He usually never let anyone
else inside this forbidden zone of his inner self, but something
about Cindy made him feel that with her it would be okay.

"I tell you, I was scared shitless!" he finished up the tale.

Cindy laughed. "Let me tell you about my first barracuda. It
wasn't as big as your shark, but I know what you felt like; I could
just feel those long rows of shiny, white teeth biting into my
rear!" And they both laughed at the image, as she launched into
her scary tale.

After the diving stories came other scary stories, as they each
related times when the waves were this high and the wind blew
that hard, and on and on. David sometimes had trouble keeping
things straight, as to when he was with his dad and when he
wasn't, and what trip it was and when, but he thought he did fine.

He was getting more comfortable with his distorted reality of
the past weeks, the longer he had someone to talk to, and he was
sometimes a bit confused about what was true. *Sort of like a parallel
universe kind of thing,* he fancied.

After both had told their best fables, they fell silent and
continued gazing at the water world about them. The sun was
overhead now and, except for the breeze reaching them on the
higher ground, they would have been very hot.

Puffball clouds danced by in an unending chorus line. Bird
songs from the green bush inland floated in and out on the wind,
providing evidence that there was, after all, some form of animal
life in the unmoving vegetation cover. Both of them were buried
in deep thought.

"Hey," David suddenly spoke up, "I know someplace you'd
love to go—at least I think you would. It's pretty neat." He
twisted in his sitting spot and faced her expectantly.

"Well, where is it? What is it?" she mocked his enthusiasm.

"Okay, it's right over there, to the south. The first… second… third cove after the one my boat is in." He pointed with an outstretched arm and she tried to follow. "Except that you can't see it from here," he added with a mischievous grin.

"Thanks, you're a big help," she replied dryly.

"That's what's so great about it," he was obviously excited; "it's sort of hidden, secret-like, and it's really small, and easy to miss the entrance."

"Okay, I believe you. So, what's special?"

David became more serious. "It's just… nice. It's so small and pretty. It's like all these other coves, except in miniature. I guess that's what's great about it." He paused and added, "It's just secret, that's all."

"Well, we'll have to go there," she tried to buoy him up again; "it does sound cute. When do we go?" She cocked her head quizzically, and waited expectantly, with hands on hips.

David looked at her sitting there—her tanned legs crossed in front, looking much like a temple statue, except for the brown hair lifting lightly in the breeze, and an impish look that no temple would allow—and he felt a warmth welling from deep within, such as he had never felt before.

He'd had rushes from other girls before, but usually that was a sexual feeling, mainly of physical attraction. This was different; it was… a mixture of trust and friendship. A desire to hold her, and wanting to be a part of her, to share everything with her. He couldn't sort any of these out from each other; they all were part of one thing, inseparable.

He stood up and reached down to take a hand. "Soon," he replied quietly. "I'll take you there when it's time."

She let herself be pulled to her feet, and didn't resist when he kept hold of her hand on their way back to the beach.

They picked up the cooler and found a slightly more secluded spot in the shade to have lunch, a little more out of the direct sightline of the ketch. "Carrie likes to use the binoculars a lot,"

Cindy had remarked with a smile, as she took the initiative to move their lunch spot.

They sat next to each other, shoulders touching, as they leaned against the trunk of a small palm. It was sort of ridiculous, the two of them trying to share the slender trunk for a backrest, but it served to place their touching in a jocular vein, and accomplished the result both wanted.

As they continued talking, David gradually became obsessed with a desire to kiss her. He knew it was absurd, seeing as how they had just met and all, but he couldn't help the thoughts racing in his head. As she gaily talked on about some of her friends in school, it was all he could do to keep from staring at her lips and wishing they would stop moving about, so he could kiss her. He kept trying to think of how he could suddenly surprise her, sort of corner her, so she'd have to let him kiss her.

He even tried a couple of moves, like when she leaned forward to get something out of the cooler, and he leaned over to be in the way when she turned around. But she would always twist out of the way somehow, as if she knew something was going on, even though her back was turned. It was getting frustrating for him, as the desire burned even more intensely with each failed attempt.

David was sure she must know what he wanted, since it soon almost became a game. Besides, when she would get excited about some story she was relating, she'd lightly place a hand on his knee for emphasis. He finally gave up on the kiss, figuring there was plenty of time for that, and settled for just the joy of being close and touching.

With lunch finished, they fell silent and simply leaned back against the tree, enjoying the satisfaction of a full belly and no responsibilities. The heat of the day was now beginning to penetrate even the shade of their small palm.

The beach was a brilliant arc of white light, and the heat waves shimmering off its surface made the meeting of water and vegetation a dancing smear of blue and green. An occasional breath of trade wind air would hit upon the water's surface and ripple out a small but expanding wave of disturbance, until it joined the full force of the wind, out past the anchored ketch, where the island no longer obstructed its path.

It was getting hotter, and David was settling more and more into a half-conscious state, when he was suddenly jerked awake by a strong pull on his arm.

"Come on, lazy! Time for a swim!"

David stared blankly at the figure standing directly above him. Cindy was grinning broadly. With one quick motion, she grabbed the bottom of her shirt with crossed arms and pulled it up and over her head. David watched the tanned band of skin rise from her belly, up the firm expanse of her stretched ribs to her rounded shoulders, and eventually the smiling face which popped out of the inside-out shirt. She tossed her head lightly to make her hair fall into place and, starting to unbutton her shorts, coyly smiled at David. "What's the matter? Disappointed I didn't forget my suit?"

David snapped his gaze up from her blue-and-white striped bikini top, to meet her eyes. "Huh? No, I was just…" he stammered.

But she didn't let him finish. She dropped her shorts, revealing long, tanned legs, and kicked them into his face with a well-placed lift of her foot. "Come on!" she called, as she ran down the short beach and dove into the transparent, light-blue water.

David didn't have a swimsuit on, but he often swam in his shorts, anyway. He could see her body gliding underwater and then pop to the surface. She turned and stood up in the shoulder-high water, waiting expectantly. David finally came to life and, pulling his shirt off, ran down the beach and dove in to join her.

He got a big splash of water in the face for a greeting when he surfaced, and the battle was on. A white froth of water boiled and leapt between the two until, finally, Cindy took advantage of an unguarded moment to quickly dive and pull David off his feet. They both tussled underwater and rose to the surface, laughing and hanging onto each other.

Slowly the laughter ceased, as they each released their hold and started to clear the water from their eyes. Finished, they stood in the clear, warm water, and grinned at each other for the fun they'd just had. Their eyes met and grins turned to tight smiles.

Cindy turned onto her back, floating, and slowly began to stroke her way along the beach, all the while looking back at David. As if pulled by the magnet of her smile, David breast-stroked after her, keeping pace with barely a ripple in the water.

They swam for a while longer, and then lay in the sun to dry off. When they could no longer bear the heat, they would again tear off to the water and swim some more. With each romp in the water they held each other more closely, and became less guarded where their hands fell and their bodies touched.

At one point, in the middle of some play, David caught Cindy in his arms, just as she was coming to the surface, and kissed her fully on the lips. She didn't resist.

Turning her back quickly to face the direction of the ketch, she scolded, with her light smile, "David! Someone might see. My sister, for one." She raised a finger to her lips and then gently placed it against his. "Later—not now," she promised, and they waded back to the beach.

23

David had a terrible time sleeping that night. He was in and out of dreams of all sorts, in particular the one with the moving shapes, and the girl whom he could never seem to catch. The last time he was in it, though, it changed slightly: the shapes were no longer purplish, but began to have a bluish cast to them, and the girl didn't have silver hair anymore, but more brownish, sort of streaked with blending golden waves. The face still had a familiar feeling about it—even though it was always changing—and he was frustrated at not being able to place it exactly. The dream never ended with him waking satisfied—there were too many unfitted pieces.

But most of the time he lay partially awake in a jumble of floating memories, images, and scenes, none of which he could hang onto for any length of time. Of course, there were the day's events with Cindy, and he re-ran those many times.

Sometimes his imagination would change things slightly, and he would be with her someplace making out, but that image wouldn't last very long before he would lose it. Reality being more intense, his thoughts would soon drift back to some other memory of the day, for him to ponder upon. Yet, put into perspective with his past, the emotions he felt were confusing.

He'd had a girlfriend back at McCaskey High. They'd been going together off and on for two years, and with each break-up and reunion, the relationship seemed to change. He and Pam got along great most of the time. They had differences, to be sure, but they could usually smooth those over. However, each time they got back together it seemed like the memories of those arguments, and the upsets at the dances and other get-togethers, stuck their ugly heads back in again, making it harder and harder to brush them away. At first, David and Pam tried to talk the problems out. That seemed to work for some of the minor disagreements, but when it came down to the more serious ones, talking turned into yelling at each other.

Scenes of those times broke into his rambling thoughts that night, and a strange dream popped up. He and Pam were arguing about something—he couldn't remember what, but it was trivial—and suddenly, before he realized it, he and Pam turned into his dad and mom; they were the ones arguing now. David wasn't anywhere around, as if he didn't even exist. Yet, he was nevertheless the one who was experiencing what his dad was feeling and thinking during the argument.

It was really strange and shook David up for a while, so much so that he had to go topside in the darkness for some cooler air, to recertify who and where he was.

Another thing confusing to him was that he had sincerely felt at the time that he loved Pam, that she would be the only one for him for the rest of his life, his wife to have and to hold forever. But she wasn't. They last broke up two months before he left, and this time he had the feeling that they wouldn't ever get back together again.

He still felt a lot of affection toward her, and cared for her, even now. As long as their dates had been well-spaced, it was terrific. But, when they started getting serious again, the arguments also started up again. The contradiction between what he felt and what he knew seemed insolvable, and David was very frustrated.

And now he was head over heels about Cindy! Could he truly feel that way about Pam and now feel the same about Cindy, only more intensely and without the fighting involved? Wasn't true love supposed to be only for one person—all-consuming, like on TV or in those mushy romance novels? Maybe something was wrong with him—weird, over-sexed, or something—but he doubted that was true.

Another question now arose, however. He and Cindy didn't argue about anything—not even a hint of the possibility. Of course, they had only just met, but it was something that nagged at him. Loving a person and fighting with them at the same time had gone together in his experience, and he had an unspoken expectation of it continuing now. He didn't want it to—he knew that—yet he had no basis of experience on which to fulfill that wish. His mom and dad fought, too, so he had it at home as well.

Except, and the thought pierced his awareness with bright clarity, *Dad and Rachel didn't—not like with my real mom, anyway.* Gregory and Rachel argued about small things, in more of a brief discussion; nothing ever got blown up into something big. It was different, somehow. That realization was intriguing to David, and he turned it over in his mind, to examine more closely.

He then smiled wryly and thought, *One of the first things I've ever seen positive about Dad marrying Rachel! Well, she is good to him,* David conceded, as memories flooded in of her holding her own in a discussion and not taking any guff, yet treating his dad with respect and tenderness.

Gregory seemed to thrive on the attention, and then feel bad when he habitually fell into the old defensive position of days past, and ended up hurting Rachel's feelings. *Yeah,* David had to admit, *Dad isn't quite the same person he used to be. And Rachel has a lot to do with it.*

It was about the time David allowed this final thought into his consciousness that he finally fell soundly asleep. But by this time, outside, a lightness to the eastern horizon had just begun to delineate the small island's jagged skyline of rocks and trees, as daylight prepared its entrance. It had been a long night.

24

Over the following days, David increasingly spent his time with Cindy. Sometimes it was as a guest aboard *Dawn Treader*, for lunch or dinner with the family; other times they all went exploring ashore, or had a barbeque on the beach. Often, he and Cindy took Carrie to the reefs on the south side for some skin-diving. Most frequently it was just the two of them, ending up filling the days exploring beaches and swimming.

It did cross his mind about her parents letting him be around so much, but they didn't seem to mind, and actually appeared glad to have Cindy occupied and out of their hair. But, regardless of how it happened, he spent every moment he could with her, since he truly had little else to do—or wanted to do.

He had an insatiable appetite for her companionship and, as far as he could tell, she wanted to be with him, too. Sometimes at night, when he was recalling the day spent with Cindy, the thought would cross his mind that she was just tolerating him because he happened to be handy, and he looked for evidence of his suspicions, but to no avail. She seemed to genuinely care for him.

But, does she love me? That was the question that plagued him whenever he was back alone on his boat. *Does she feel the same as me? How can I find out?* He went over the matter again and again, and one day finally decided he had to find out.

He arrived at Cindy's boat in the early afternoon. She was sitting on the deck reading a book and waved at him when he drew near. "Hi," he greeted her cheerfully. "Let's go somewhere for a while. It's time you saw my secret place," he added, mysteriously.

"Right! I won't tell a soul," she grinned, as she joined the play. "Just a minute, though—I've got to clear things with headquarters." And she scooted below deck to find her mom. In a moment she was back. "Let's go."

Since it took about twenty minutes to get there by rowing, David decided to use some of his remaining outboard fuel. Neither of them spoke much as they went along, preferring instead to just stare at the seabed pass rapidly beneath or look for nesting birds on the headlands they passed.

When they were almost there, David asked, "See anything?" and looked expectantly at Cindy. She shook her head and they continued. A minute later he asked again. Still she couldn't see anything unusual.

Finally, David had to turn the dinghy straight at the rocky bluff looming above them, or he would miss the opening. Then she cried out, "Now I see it! There's a break in the rocks here. Show off!" she teased.

They made a quick right turn, back again, and they were in the tiny cove. It was only about a hundred feet wide in the cove, though the water was nearly twenty feet deep, and the cliffs on either side were almost as high as the water was deep. In the back was a tiny sand beach, where a few trees and bushes had taken root above the waterline. It was almost entirely closed off by the gray limestone cliffs, except for the entrance and a steep slope behind the trees.

With the motor off, the dinghy drifted a few feet further and stopped. The only sound was the gentle lapping of the wavelets against the rock. Cindy slowly turned to take it all in and stopped at David, who was grinning proudly.

"We've been by here several times, and I didn't notice that opening. And you never told, either," she scolded.

"Of course not; I said I'd show you when it was time."

"And that's now, right?"

"Yup."

"Okay, let's get ashore." They both took an oar and paddled the few strokes to the beach.

After pulling the dinghy up the beach a little, they both habitually glanced along the beach for anything interesting, then settled at the top, near a large piece of driftwood which had somehow found its way into the cove. They both sat facing the water, David with his legs drawn up and resting his arms on his knees, and Cindy cross-legged, as she toyed with a couple of small shells she had just picked up.

"You like my place?" David finally broke the silence.

"Yes, I like your place," she smiled softly at him. "It's nice. Nice and quiet, and small. Small enough... to be called your own."

"That's what I think, too," he smiled back, and then fiddled with the sand. "You like me, too?" He waited for her answer.

Cindy didn't respond immediately. She pulled her knees up and hugged them, looking over at him. "Yes, I like you, too."

"Do you love me?"

"Well, now, that's a little more serious of a question," she smiled tightly. "After all, we've only just met, really—under two weeks ago!"

"Yes, but... sometimes you know something is right in only a little time."

"Well, I do think that's true... sometimes."

"Yeah, I know it sounds like a serious question... but, I mean... could it be more than just liking me—maybe just a little more? Like... really, *really* liking someone?"

"I could ask the same question." She paused. "There are all kinds of love. I love my mom and dad... even Carrie," she grinned. "I have friends I love and enjoy spending time with. And then there's love with a lot of commitment to the relationship—a lot of caring for each other. There are many different kinds of love."

David waited.

"So, love can be a serious word… or just a way of telling a person you feel more than simply liking them."

David listened carefully. "Okay, in that way. Liking them a lot. Hugely," he grinned. "But, more than just liking… wanting to spend more time together—lots of time, at the least," he quickly added. "So, in that way, I love you." He waited again.

She was amused by his eager face, as his feelings played openly upon it. "Alright, in that way of caring about someone a lot, and wanting to spend time together, I can say that I love you, too," she gave in with a tight smile. "Happy now?"

They were the words David had been waiting, aching for. She loved him—even in that qualified meaning, he didn't care!

He reached over, gently touched her face, and ran his hand down over her hair, lightly streaked in golden waves from exposure to the sun. He then pulled her over to him and brought his face to hers—a glance, eye to eye, then the softness of a kiss. A rush of warmth passed between them as he cradled her head in his hands, and their kisses strengthened in intensity, their bodies now pressing together. She felt so soft and warm against him, so alive, so giving of herself. She made David feel as though something was falling from him, like shedding a skin which had outgrown its usefulness.

Deep within he felt a stirring, not just of passion newly found, but a stirring sense of his person, of who he was. It was something changing—of him losing something and gaining in return. What it was, he had no idea, and at the moment he couldn't have cared less.

After a few moments, the heat of the sun reflected from the beach began to take its toll. Cindy released herself from David's embrace and rolled back, smiling at him. Beads of perspiration formed on her brow and where their bodies had touched.

"It's too hot for this," she stated abruptly. David stared at her without understanding. "I mean, let's cool off," she explained and sat up.

David started to say something about not wearing a suit, and she interrupted with a laugh, "Well, who needs a swimming suit?" She raised her eyebrows, and her mouth formed that tight little grin. David never quite knew what to make of her intentions when she did that. He could never tell if she was being serious, or what.

He suddenly threw his usual hesitancy away. "Alright. Who needs suits?"

"So, turn your back and drop your shorts," she laughed as she turned, and glanced back to see if he was doing likewise.

David turned and started undressing. Strange, it didn't seem like an unusual thing to do, as though he had been skinny-dipping all his life. Truly, he had only done it twice before, and that was at midnight with some of the guys, when they were camping at the lake. But this seemed like the most natural thing in the world to do now—no suit, go nude.

He heard the sand crunch behind him: footsteps. Almost finished undressing, he turned in time to see Cindy running the few feet to the water. A thin, white line ran across her back and a small triangle on her seat marked the outlines of her suit, contrasting with the brown smoothness which formed the rest of her agile body. David watched her splash into the shallows and then dive in. Youth becoming a woman, he marveled at the beauty of what he saw. In a moment, he too was churning the shallow water and splashing toward her.

They played their usual teasing and splashing games, swimming along the shore and then out into the middle of the small circle of water, treading water and catching their breath, watching each other's bobbing, smiling, wet heads all the while.

"Wow, this feels so good!" she exclaimed.

David had to agree. It had been getting pretty uncomfortable there on the beach.

"I love this little place." She twisted about, turning a full circle. "I feel I could stay here forever."

"Me, too. The rest of the world and all the problems don't seem to fit, and can't intrude," he added.

They drifted closer together in the clear blue water. Their eyes rambled about the enclosure they were in and stopped on each other. They were very close to one another now.

"I love you," David said softly, as he treaded water to maintain his position.

"And I love you."

Slowly they drew together, and their lips met as they embraced each other. Their bodies touched lightly as they slipped beneath the surface and slowly sank. The feeling David had at that instant was somehow familiar, enchanting, yet comforting. It was like... floating in a big blue cloud which obscures everything you want to see. Except that this time he didn't need to see; he had in his arms all that he wanted, all that he had been seeking.

The floating, the blue, the girl... it all suddenly came to him: *My dream, it's my dream! But now it's no dream—it's real.*

And the reality of a need for air was there, too. "Ah-h!" Cindy exploded, as she emerged on the surface with David. "I thought I was going to pop!"

David laughed as he caught his breath. "But didn't you like it?"

She nodded with a smile.

"Ever kiss like that before?"

She shook her head.

"Me neither. Want to do it again?" he teased.

"Silly," she smiled, and slowly swam toward shore.

Side by side, they both emerged from the water and went to their clothes. David slipped on his shorts and tossed his shirt over to Cindy. "Want to use this to dry off?"

Momentarily holding her shirt to her front, above her shorts, she turned to him. "Okay, thanks," and she turned slightly away from him, as she toweled her hair with his shirt. David watched her, intrigued with the womanly ritual and the way her small shoulders worked, as she rubbed the shirt and her hair between her hands. Twice he glimpsed the gently curved flesh of her breasts. Finished, she turned and handed the shirt back.

"You're peeking," she lightly admonished him.

"I'm not peeking. I'm just watching," he replied quietly.

Her own shirt again covering her front, she softly answered, "I don't mind," and turned to pull it over her head.

25

They climbed the short, steep slope at the head of the small cove, to where a cooling breeze could reach them, and found a shady spot under a couple of twisted, wind-stunted trees. They formed a sort of canopy on the leeward side, and under this Cindy and David had a shaded view of the tiny harbor just below them. They were still slightly wet from the swim, but the dry air of the breeze was rapidly taking care of that.

They sat silently for a few moments, recovering from the exertion of the swim and the brief climb. The gnarled roots of the trees provided convenient backrests, and the two of them snuggled comfortably, half against the trees and half against each other. The warm, dry air and penetrating weariness caused both of them to drift off into their separate worlds of thought.

Cindy finally broke the silence. "Why did you want to go on your trip?"

His mind wandering and dulled by threatening sleep, David lethargically replied, "It wasn't my idea. My dad wanted to take the trip." Awakening more to the import of his answer, he quickly added, "He wanted me to go, is what I meant." He paused. "Maybe it's something he had wanted to do as a kid, and now wanted to see me do it," he extended the answer, picking up on something Dennis had mentioned yesterday, concerning himself when he was a young man. David hoped it sounded sensible.

"But that doesn't explain why you'd go along with it. That's quite a responsibility to undertake when you don't want to do it.

You could have just refused to go; he couldn't make you sail the boat."

"No, but it was pretty important to him. I had to go."

"So, you must like your dad quite a lot," she concluded and looked over at David.

"Yeah, I guess. I don't know." He was beginning to feel defensive and getting irritable. "It was just something that had to be done," he concluded. "Could we talk about something else?"

Cindy watched him for a moment. "Sure." She paused and added, "But I think this is something you should talk about."

"What do you mean?"

"I mean that I think there's something you're not telling me."

"I answered your question. What more do you want?" His voice rose and became harsh; familiar patterns of the past seemed to be enveloping them.

"Don't get angry."

"I'm not angry," he retorted, and turned away to stare off into the distance. He felt a hand reach over to pull his down from where it was, cupped under his chin. Cindy firmly resisted his reluctance and pulled him to face her.

"Look, I'm not trying to hurt you. I'm not trying to make you angry. I just want to... well, share your thoughts. If you say you love and care for me—and I do care for you—then we have to share, not only physically but our thoughts as well. If we don't do that then it won't work. Love is sharing, after all."

David kept his pout and struggled to do as she said, but it was hard. He didn't have much practice in it, either with Pam or his parents. Come to think of it, he couldn't remember much about ever sharing his innermost thoughts with anyone.

He had always visualized himself as a body with a shell about it—a shell which cracked occasionally and was quickly patched up, but also a shell that grew thicker each year. He knew that the shell would become impenetrable if he didn't do something someday, and he didn't want it to be that way. Yet, he didn't know how to stop cementing up the cracks and making them stronger. *Well, maybe this is the time to do something. The time to take a chance.*

His throat tightened up and he trembled slightly, as the shell crazed and the cracks opened wider. He looked at Cindy closely, trying to see beyond the expectant eyes and reassuring smile—the tenderness which radiated from her face.

He looked closely, to find any hint of expression which would bring back memories he had of Pam, or of what he so often saw on his mother's face, when she fought with his dad so many years ago. But his scrutiny was in vain.

"I lied," he murmured.

Cindy leaned closer. "I didn't hear you, David."

The second time it was easier. He cleared his throat and looked hesitantly into her eyes. "I lied… I lied to you—to you and your family—about how I got here… I mean, how I ended up out here… alone."

Cindy's eyes grew wide and her brow deeply furrowed, in anticipation and astonishment. "You lied to us? I don't understand. What's going on? What's with the you-being-alone part?" Her anger and confusion were clearly apparent in her rising voice and flushed face.

"Just a minute," he croaked, as he fought the welling tears which threatened to undo his anticipated relief at finally getting his tale told.

Cindy was still waiting, slowly simmering. "Okay, take your time, but I need to know the truth… about everything," she added sternly.

David took a deep breath and cleared his throat again. The tightness was receding, but gradually. He looked off, away from her, and continued, "My dad and I were sailing from Florida, just like I said. And I had finished school earlier, too, as I said. In fact, everything I said was pretty accurate—I just left out my dad." He stopped.

Cindy pulled his arm to get his attention, and turn him to face her. "Now," her voice softening but firm, "tell me. Why did you leave your dad out? What happened?"

His throat tightened again, and he struggled hard to speak. "We were… we were coming down from Georgetown, Bahamas, and it was night—really dark out. I was down below sleeping; he was in the cockpit. When I woke up, early in the morning…" he could hardly speak, as tears welled in his eyes, "he was gone. He was just gone!" His voice trembled and tears slowly slid down his cheeks. "He must have fallen overboard," he croaked.

"Oh, my god!" she burst out, hands clasped to her face, horrified at the vision of the dark, vast sea swallowing Gregory. "And… what happened to him?" She struggled with the words, but had to ask.

"He was found by another boat… two days later… A long time to be out there…" David managed to get out.

Relieved about the outcome but concerned about David, Cindy pulled him closer to her and grasped him by the shoulders. "And you feel that it's your fault it happened?"

David jerked away, angry, tears streaming, "Yes, it is! He asked me to stand watch for him earlier, so he could get some sleep," he fairly shouted. "But I was too sleepy. Too damned lazy to get out of bed!"

She let the stifled sobs come, and waited, before pulling his hand to hers. "You can't blame yourself. Accidents happen. It's easy to look back and see what could have been done differently."

"But it was me!" he blurted out in anguish. "It was my fault! I was too lazy to get up. It could have been prevented if it wasn't for how I am. And then…" he threw up his hands in disgust, "and then, when I did realize what had happened, do you think I could turn the boat around and search for him? Do you? Hell, no!" he spit the words out. "I didn't know how to sail the damn boat! I made some stupid tries but failed. I'd been too lazy all those years, when he tried to teach me, too stubborn to pay attention and learn how to sail well, so I could help him." And, as he said "help", David broke into heaving sobs.

Cindy pulled him to her tightly and laid his head on her chest, stroking his hair and waiting for what was next to come.

All the pent-up tension, all the withheld recrimination, all the disgust with himself was releasing and flowing from his body. He had played at being an adult for long enough—now he needed some mothering. And Cindy was there to comfort him.

But it wasn't just release from the accident that was pouring forth, it was also an outpouring of his inner self. The shell about himself was now permanently shattered, not completely, but the cracks could never again be solidly sealed against the emotions which wanted out or in. He could feel it happening—a vaguely familiar sensation, except that before it had only been imagined and not experienced.

It was as though his skin was bursting and falling from him, as a new person emerged—like him yet not like him. He struggled against the bonds of resistance, and tentatively touched the fabric of his newfound emotional freedom—freedom from his childhood, from his old self. He no longer felt alone.

The comfort of Cindy's body was immensely satisfying to David. He let her hold him tightly as he clung to her, the rise and fall of her bosom against his head seeming to drain away his anguish with every breath. Her body smelled of the pure sweetness of skin, warmed by the sun and newly cleansed by the sea. His breathing slowed and the tears stopped.

Presently, Cindy gently released her clasp and turned herself, so that he lay on his back with his head cradled in her lap. She gazed gently down at him. "Feel better?" He nodded yes.

"You just can't blame yourself for all that happened. So you were an ornery kid who didn't want to learn how to operate some dumb boat? Is that so unusual? Do kids always do what their parents want them to do?"

David forced a faint smile back.

"Look, I'm a pretty stubborn person when I want to be, and I've been stubborn with my parents and regretted it later. But they expect a certain amount of stubbornness, and we expect them to expect it, so we give them what they expect." She smiled at David, and he grinned slightly at her logic.

"We can't help being kids any more than they can help being adults; we each do what is part of us. It's hard to change that sort of thing," she concluded.

"Yeah, but we can't be kids all the time. We've got to grow up sometime. And I should have started way back when," David protested.

"Well, that's true. It's hard to know when it's time to start growing up, though. I mean, how do we know when we're supposed to stop acting like a kid and act like an adult?"

"Well, I know one time for certain, now," David scowled.

"Hey," she stroked his head, "of course you do *now*. Hindsight is great; foresight is the tough one." She was silent for a moment. "I guess all we can do is our best, and keep trying when we fail."

With his tears now drying on his face, David grinned despite himself. "Now, where have I heard that one before?" They both laughed lightly.

They remained there a while longer, she playing with his hair and leaning down for an occasional kiss, each buried in common thoughts.

"How do you think he managed to be found by another boat," Cindy carefully brought the subject back.

"I thought about that. The rescue gear was gone—it has to be pulled out by someone in the water—so he would float and attract attention. Our location at the time wasn't exactly off the beaten track, either, and that probably helped." He was silent for a moment. "It was so dark out there, though, and all that sea. And the thought of him out there in it, calling for me to help him… and I…"

"Okay, enough already. There wasn't anything to be done at the time—I'm sure he knew that. Your father seems to be a good seaman and a good person; I'm sure he won't blame you for what you couldn't do."

David was glad to hear what she said, since her reasoning was what he had eventually clawed his way to figuring out. But it was still hard to get past the emotions surrounding the logic.

"I know it's hard for you to tell someone, to uncork the bottle you've put it in, but you have to do that… and you did!" She smiled brightly and caressed his forehead, planting a light kiss. David wiped an eye with the back of his hand and managed a slight smile. "So, tell me all about his being found." And she settled back for the story.

He then told her in detail about the fishermen he had stumbled upon, and their conversation about someone matching his dad being found a few days earlier, out to sea in the area he fell overboard. David emphasized how sure they were of the person being alive and taken someplace.

Cindy intently watched David become increasingly heartened, as he told his story and ended it. She studied the radiant confidence of his face, paused thoughtfully, then joined his mood and smiled coyly. "Well, if he's safe at home by now, he's probably sitting there worried about what happened to you. It works both ways, you know."

David pulled himself upright. "Christ, I never thought of that. I've always looked at it from my end. Maybe he is. Wouldn't that be something? Here I've been, worrying about him, and he's been worrying about me!" They both laughed.

"What about your mom? She'd be worried about you, too."

David snorted, "Rachel? She's not my mom; she's my stepmother."

"So? She's still a human with feelings, and I bet she cares what happens to you, regardless of what you think of her," Cindy shot back.

David didn't say anything. But she wasn't going to let him get away without explaining himself.

"Why do you dislike her so much? Honestly?"

David thought and replied, "I don't know. But she shouldn't be there; she just doesn't belong."

"What do you mean, 'belong'?"

"Well… hell, I don't know," he picked up a rock and threw it out toward the water. It fell far short. "I guess I used the wrong word, because she does fit in a way. She fits with my dad a lot better than my real mom, that's for sure."

"But not with you."

"Not with me."

"Does she try?"

"Yeah," he replied, after a pause.

"Do you?"

"Nope."

"That's not fair, you know?" Cindy continued, after collecting her thoughts for a moment.

"I suppose not." It was the first time he had even allowed that much. "But… well, it's hard."

"Because she's not your real mom?"

He nodded.

"Well, now, is that the way you divide the world up—the real people and the ones who aren't, because they had the misfortune not to be the first ones?"

He didn't get what she was driving at.

"How about me? Am I a real one?"

"Of course you are."

"You mean to tell me you never had a girlfriend before?"

"Not like you. You're… special." He hated the difficulty he had in finding the right words.

"Come on, how about a little honesty? Weren't any of those girls special at the time? Be honest, damn it. Be honest with yourself."

Her sharp voice pulled his face toward her. She was in control of her emotions, but obviously put out at him. "Well," he stammered. And Pam jumped to mind. He couldn't lie about her. "Yeah, they were at the time."

"So, after the first one, none of the rest are real, including me?"

"No," he snapped back, "you're mixing it all up. You're real to me. You're—"

"Look," Cindy interrupted, and laid a hand on his knee, "all I'm trying to do is point out that you might be a little unfair to yourself, and to other people at the same time. I'm not the first one, but that doesn't make me any less important to you now, does it?"

David shook his head.

"Okay. The main thing is how we get along with each other, and what we mean to each other. Right?"

She felt his anger evaporating in the cooling breeze. "Now, since Rachel isn't the first one, it doesn't make her any less valuable as a mother to you just on that basis. And you already admitted she fits better as a wife for your dad."

It seemed to make sense, David had to agree, but the years of resentment wouldn't let the emotion die. Yet the way Cindy had put it, comparing herself with Rachel, had a powerful effect; something about that rang out clear, through the fog which tried to cover it up. Although an exact awareness of what she was saying and an immediate acceptance escaped him, that comparison—that image—stayed.

"David?"

Her voice brought him back. "Huh? What?"

"Do you understand what I'm saying?"

"Yeah, I think so; I know what you're saying. It's just that it's hard to make it fit. I need some time to put it together."

Cindy smiled. "Well, there's lots of that around here."

David smiled too, glad to have the gloom slipping away.

"Hey," she started to stand up, "I told my mom I'd only be gone for a little while, and it's been almost three hours already." She tugged at him to get going.

David groaned, "Okay, okay. I'm coming," and finished the job of getting up.

"I do care for you… a lot. You understand that?" She looked closely into his eyes. Receiving a nod, she kissed him lightly, and they set off toward the beach and dinghy.

26

On the way back to Dawn Treader, Cindy asked about him telling her mom and dad about the accident.

But David quickly replied with a decisive, "No." He wasn't ready yet. It had been hard enough telling her, let alone some adults. What would they think of…? No, he just couldn't handle it yet.

When he got back aboard *Endeavor*, it seemed as if every part of the cabin inside had eyes and was watching his every move: the clock on the bulkhead, the open cabin door, the chart table, the sink drain yawning at him… everything. They seemed to be accusing him of letting out the secret that only he and the boat had shared. It was a breach of trust to let someone else in on it.

Yet, the longer he sat at the nav station, the more he felt the boat wasn't angry with him, just curious. Curious to see what he would do now that their secret was out. Wondering about this recently acquired master, measuring him against the departed one.

Was there a boy or a man in charge here? Would he kick the boat and throw tools at it, as the boy did not so long ago, for not doing exactly what he wanted—even though he didn't set its rudder nor trim its sails, so that the orders could be followed? Or would he follow the father, and learn what the boat could teach him, not only about how to make it fly and sing, but also how to discipline himself, to realize the depth of his hidden abilities? It had taught the father; could it teach the son?

David felt the voices of the boat talking. He saw his father sitting in the nav seat, right where he now was. His father was looking at the charts, thinking, planning, hoping.

Hoping what? Hoping that his son would someday be seated there, in command of the small ship, carrying on from his own late start in the mysteries of the sail. *What is it he wants from me?* What does any father wish from his child? *What would I wish from my child?*

And, with that last question, David began to understand that the answers were beginning to come to him. The answers to all the questions would unfold over the next few days—he just had to remain open to them. But it would be hard to follow the path.

A warmth enveloped David, as the voices ceased and the image of his father dissolved into him. At least he wouldn't be alone, not on this ship—and perhaps never again.

The ancient dream came again that night: the billowing, blue, cloudlike shapes of color; the mist drifting among the trees... David walked—floated—through the changing shapes. He was still looking for something, but now he knew what it was: the young woman. Several times she came that night, each visit becoming more distinct, until at last Cindy stood clearly before him.

His Cindy, to be sure, but somehow different, too. And he knew her name and called to her, and often she would hear, but not always. Sometimes they would meet, and touch, and walk together, as the shapes moved about them.

Despite this moment of beauty, there was a problem which haunted them both: there seemed to be no way out. The forest was endless and the rolling shapes kept them off balance, so that when progress had been made in one direction, they would end up back where they began. It was extremely frustrating.

And when David awoke in the morning, the frustration carried through.

"You're sure grumpy today," Cindy chided him after lunch. "Anything I should know about?"

He shrugged his shoulders. "Naw, I just didn't sleep so well last night, that's all."

They were sitting out on the bow of the ketch. During the night, some high, thin clouds had come in from the northwest and were still there that morning, including some puffy ones which grew with the sunrise. Off to the southwest, thunderclouds gathered on the horizon, and the two of them could see occasional streaks of lightning against the grayness, as the clouds moved along the horizon. A shift of wind to the west indicated unsettled weather for a day or so. It was a nice change from the usual beating heat, and nobody seemed to mind.

"Been thinking about our talk yesterday?" Cindy filled in the words which fit the thoughts in his mind.

"Yeah…," he drawled the answer.

"Any conclusions?"

"Nope," he deadpanned, then smiled slightly. "Not any really big ones. I guess I've made some little ones, though."

"Like what?" she encouraged.

David had no idea which ones; he simply had this feeling that some things were settled, that was all. He sat for a moment, thinking.

"I guess about my dad. It doesn't seem like he'd be so angry with me now. Not just for sort of abandoning him back there—I think he'd understand the problems involved—but more for me having been such a hard-ass about everything for the last few years, ever since he married Rachel. No, even before that."

He looked blankly down at his hands. "I don't know when it started, but I just wasn't very cooperative… about anything. I can see that now, admit it, and be ashamed of it. But I'm not going to let it get me down; I'm going to do better from now on. It was really childish to act that way.

"And that's why I don't think he'd be angry now… because I realize what I've been doing and I'm going to 'keep on plugging away', as he always put it. That's what I think would please him."

He thought, and smiled. "To see that after all these years of effort, he's finally making some progress on my thick skull. And I don't mind it. I was wrong."

"You were also a kid, don't forget," Cindy put in. "Some things you just can't help when you're a kid, such as your parents getting a divorce," she added.

"But now I can, right? Isn't that what being an adult is about, or at least part of it? Being able to..." he sought the way to put it, "...carry on, regardless of what's happened, whether in the past or just yesterday?" He paused. "Or just a few weeks ago? I mean, I admit it, I had a lot to learn about carrying on, even though I refused to learn what my dad was trying to teach me for all those years. And I didn't like facing up to it one bit. It wasn't much fun, I'll tell you." He glanced away and watched the thunderclouds for a moment.

"But I did it. I didn't give up; I kept going. And I learned a lot—about the boat, but also about me. So, part of me died out there and another part took its place." He stopped abruptly, as a thought blossomed.

"What?" Cindy peered quizzically at him.

"You know, it's funny. I was going to say that I grew up, but that doesn't seem to fit. Then I remembered last night, at the nav station, when I sort of saw—well, felt—my father being there with me. And then he sort of dissolved into me. I just now remembered that, and also several other times on the trip when it seemed like my dad was there helping me. Except that it wasn't like it was another person—more like he and I were in the same space together, working.

"So, when I was going to say that I grew up, it suddenly dawned on me that this new part was... my dad. I've become like him, at least in some ways, like being able to handle the boat—better, anyway—and now facing up to things and going on, regardless of how hard it is. He was very good at that."

David rolled the discovery over in his mind, like a curious

shell picked up at low tide.

"Humph!" he grunted in amazement. "All of his trying to teach me, by taking classes and doing other stuff, couldn't do it. But he still managed to get to me—through the boat; he and the boat together, like a trap I'd stepped into. I had to do it their way or I'd never survive, no doubt. I had to grow up, be an adult, like him." David paused to collect his thoughts, as Cindy quietly sat waiting.

"The boat was just like a part of him. He spent hours and hours working on it, fixing it so it worked smoother. So, I never really was alone out here, after all. Dad was there, just in a different form." David drifted off with his thoughts again.

He grinned suddenly and exclaimed, "Dad got to me after all!" He mused on this and then remembered Cindy. "You probably think I'm crazy."

"No, not at all," she reassured him. "I don't quite follow all of it, since I haven't been in your shoes and know all that happened, but it does make sense. I mean, we all have to grow up sometime, and often it takes a crisis like yours. And, whether we like it or not, we all have part of our parents in us, too. How could we not help it, with them being around all the time…?

"Like now—hi, Mom."

"Sorry to interrupt," Colleen apologized, as she walked along the deck toward them, "but I thought maybe you two might like some lemonade." She held up two glasses.

"Sure," they responded, and gladly took the drinks. Colleen returned to the companionway hatch and disappeared below.

A cool gust of air from the west made them look around behind them, to see a very large thunderhead not far away. It was moving rapidly toward them, sunlit streaks of rain pouring below it, but the squall would probably miss.

"I think you've done pretty well figuring things out, for being such a thick-skulled kid," Cindy teased.

David grinned, genuinely pleased with himself. "Yeah, I guess so." He took a deep breath and stretched. "I sure feel one heck of a lot better, that's for sure!"

The roll of distant thunder could now be heard, and the spectacle grew closer.

"How come you never have any problems?" David protested.

"Did I say that?"

"No, but you seem to get along so well with your family, and they're all pretty nice."

"And that means I shouldn't have any difficulties in my life?"

"No."

"Well, let's just say that I've had my problems, too. Just because my family is fairly normal doesn't mean that I don't have arguments with my parents or sister. I've got my ideas about how grown up I am, and how much freedom I should have for making my own decisions; that's still the biggest source of disagreements.

"Every kid has that problem to go through, whether you've just got two parents or only one—or three, or four. That's just part of growing up—or so my mother frequently reminds me," she added with her curious little smile, and David had to grin back. "We've all got to work through our own particular situation. Nobody's exempt."

A huge drop of water landed square on Cindy's forehead, as if punctuating the end of her last statement. They both looked up and then behind them, at the huge, dark cloud they saw earlier. The blackness was almost upon them, and a further chill swept the air. The sound of raindrops hitting the water, making little plopping sounds, was all about them, and the tempo of their percussion rapidly increased, as the main wall of rain sped forward. David and Cindy barely made it to the cockpit before the squall hit.

The ketch quickly swung into the cool wind, which now made the rigging hum, and the sheets of rain drummed loudly on the decks and bimini top. Thunder cracked sharply and lightning lit up the dancing water about them, as the cloud doused them in its shadow.

Cindy and David, along with the whole family, watched fascinated in the protection of the bimini cover, as the squall rolled over them, over the parched beach and island, and on out to sea.

In twenty minutes it was all over, and the wet decks began to steam as the sun poked through the trailing clouds.

Everyone had a great time watching the show, and now sat in the cockpit chatting about memorable details. Dennis finally changed the subject, by off-handedly commenting, "Nice to be where we are when one of those comes around. Won't be so much fun when we're out there sailing in a couple of days."

David was taken completely by surprise. Despair furrowing his brow, he glanced at Cindy. She was surprised as well.

"Are we leaving?"

Dennis looked at her and smiled. "Well, we can't stay here forever, though it wouldn't be too bad a place, but we've got to move on. We need to be in St. Thomas by the fifteenth to meet the Ackermans. Remember? They're going to cruise the Virgins with us for a week."

Of course she remembered, and nodded her head, but it was obvious that she had other things on her mind.

"Your mother and I were talking about it last night. We've already stayed here longer than we planned… since you seemed to be having such a good time." He winked at her and smiled at David. "So, it's about time. The wind should be back in the northeast late tomorrow, and the next day we could leave for Puerto Rico, and then go on to the Virgins."

And, with that, the conversation turned to other topics.

Although she didn't look directly at him, Cindy could tell that David was having a tough time holding up his end of the conversation from then on. She sneaked her hand over to his and gave it a gentle squeeze.

27

Endeavor needed her hull scrubbed, to get off most of the sea growth so that she would sail faster, and Cindy had offered to help David with the chore. It took about an hour, not because the area to be covered was so large, but because they had to dive down with masks and fins to reach most of it, and that meant a lot of breath-holding. They'd scrub for five or ten minutes, rest for three, and then go at it again.

Of course, it wasn't all solid work. They managed to find numerous ways to distract each other, such as a brush accidentally running onto David's hand or head, or Cindy mysteriously losing a fin.

But the job was finally done and they lay on the cabin top, arms and legs loosely akimbo, drying in the sun and warm breeze.

They were both happy, lying there letting the air play about their wet bodies, and the sun, like a sponge, soak up what remained of their energy. It had been a good time, despite the work involved. As Dennis had predicted, the weather was settling—with mostly clear skies, and only a few banks of thunderclouds on the horizon—and the wind was beginning to come out of the northeast.

Flopping over onto her stomach, Cindy laid her head on her crossed arms and looked at David. "So, what now?"

David was still on his back. He rolled his head and sleepily opened one eye. "What do you mean, 'what now'?"

"I mean, what are you going to do after we get to Puerto Rico? What are you going to do after that?" And she added, after a pause, "What are you and I going to do?"

David lolled his head back up and closed his eyes. "I don't want to think about it."

"Well, I don't, either, but—"

"Hey," he interrupted, as he rolled over and wriggled next to her, "I meant I don't want to think about it right now." He reached and kissed her on her forehead, her nose, and her lips. She responded, and they lay in a tender embrace for a few moments, as the wind and sun danced upon their snuggled bodies, giving their touch a special blessing of innocent pleasure.

Easing the embrace, Cindy lay on her back and smiled. "Is it time to think about it now?"

David grinned and looked down the length of her outstretched body, legs crossed and both arms lifted overhead, cradling her head, her tanned figure taut and firm. David felt possessive of that body, wanting to share it and the spirit that lived within, joining with her physically and in mind, forever. But, how?

"Yeah, I guess it's time." They both waited for the answers to come forth. "Which one first? Which answer?" he teased, as he stalled. Cindy gave him an exasperated look.

"Okay, I get the point. Well, let's see. What will I do? Hmm… I guess I could go on to the Virgin Islands with you guys, but that would just get the boat farther from home, Pennsylvania, and I don't know if that's what Dad would want. On the other hand, I could go back to the Turks and Caicos—if I could hit them," he joked about his navigation ability, "or even go on to the Bahamas, and maybe meet Dad at one of those places. I couldn't miss all of those islands!"

Cindy smiled back and waited.

"But if I went back, I'd have to tell your parents about… the accident. They've already asked about meeting my folks in the Virgins, since they're going there, too." He grimaced at the complications of the web he had spun.

"You don't want to tell them, right?" She looked at him earnestly.

"No, not really. I like your folks a lot, and I trust them; I'm sure they'd probably understand."

Cindy gave a small nod of agreement.

"But I think this is something I'd rather handle by myself. I guess it's that if I told them, being adults they'd take over, and I'd be put in the role of a kid again, having someone else make plans to bail me out of my mess. They'd regard me as somebody needing help, not as someone who's making their way, even with the difficulties.

"I don't know," he paused and turned to Cindy. "Does that make sense?"

"Of course it does," she chided, then grew more serious to match David's mood. "I understand what you're saying.

"It's just like last summer, when I went to stay with a girlfriend in Fort Lauderdale. Somehow we crossed wires and, after I got to her parents' house, no one was there. The neighbors said the family wouldn't be back for three days—on vacation.

"So, what was I to do? Call Mommy and cry for help? Not on your life! I got a taxi, found a room at a hotel on the beach, and had a great time for three days. Then I showed up at my friend's house as if nothing had happened. When I told her what I did, she about flipped. But I never told her parents, or mine." She thought for a minute, then added, "I suppose I will someday, when I'm a lot older.

"But the point of the whole thing was handling it myself. I admit I was scared of how to go about getting a room," she chuckled at the memory of her fear, "and what if somebody molested me? But I managed and came out better for it. At least, I think I did," she added.

David enjoyed her story, but more so enjoyed the comfort of knowing he wasn't alone in this decision-making business. She was waiting for him to go on.

"So," he took a deep breath, "I guess maybe I'd better go to Puerto Rico with you guys. It's not that far away and is convenient, and I could phone home from San Juan. Besides, that way our boats could travel together at least that far, and I'd get to see you again—for a little bit, anyway."

"I'm sure my folks would be glad to have you sail along with us. They sort of worry about you, anyway. You know how parents are."

David smiled and inwardly welcomed the concern, and the relief there would be in having another boat along with him. Although he had brave talk and intentions, he was not kidding himself as to how good a seaman he was—at least at present.

"That way," Cindy continued, "it would seem natural for you to stop off at San Juan with us, and then we'd sail on—you know, to call your parents for any last-minute changes, before meeting them in St. Thomas," she completed the details of the developing plan.

"Yeah, that's true," David agreed. "That would make sense. Okay, that's how it will be then." He was relieved to have that settled and rolled over onto his back, contentedly looking up at the puffy clouds drifting overhead.

28

"And what about the other question?" Cindy queried.

David had trouble shifting thoughts, but quickly switched tracks. "Oh, yes, that question." He rolled over onto his side again, and propped his head up with an arm. "I could ask you the same thing, you know."

She nodded.

"It's both of us, after all."

"But I asked first," she teased, and her eyes searched his face.

"Okay," he sighed, and looked first at her, then out at the islands and water. "Well, you should know by now how I feel. I think we get along great, not like my old girlfriend, Pam. We talked about that." He glanced at her waiting face. "I love you very much. I feel like I want to be with you forever."

"But forever is a long time," Cindy broke in, then smiled. "I know that sounds silly… of course it is. But what I mean is, being with a person—like a wife or a husband—all their lives isn't an easy thing to do." Both of their minds recalled the recent discussions they'd had about divorce, past girlfriends and boyfriends, and step-parents.

Cindy continued, "Do you know that you could live with me that way, day after day?"

David nodded quickly.

"Well, maybe you do and maybe you don't. I'm not sure, myself. I think I could, but then this isn't exactly how life would be in the future," she gestured with one hand to the shimmering water and blazing white beach nearby. They both smiled at the contrast. "Real life is a lot different, and maybe we wouldn't get along then."

"I think we would," David stubbornly insisted.

Cindy reached over and kissed his forehead. "I think we would, too," she said softly, "but I want to be sure. And that means time—time to think and time to grow up some more. You've got a year of high school left and then college, and I'm starting this fall."

David was quiet.

"And then jobs to find, so we've got some experience and financial stability."

"But that's a long time. I'd know long before then," David protested.

"I'm just pointing out what the next steps are. I'm not saying that we won't… know before then—I don't want to be an old maid, after all," she joked. "But, at the same time, I don't want to jump into something I'm not ready for. I'm not going to exchange my parents' control over my life for a situation where my husband or the marriage puts me into an inferior position. Once I'm out from under my parents, I don't want to go back.

"I want a marriage where I'm an equal partner, sharing the work involved and the rewards, too. Look at your dad's first marriage: you told me your mom was always complaining about being second-rate, not having any opportunity to do the things she had always wanted to do. And now with Rachel things are different, right? They share, as equals."

David had to agree. Rachel put her foot down, quietly but firmly, when his dad fell into the old habit of trying to order his wife around. His mom put up with it for years, until she had finally had it with his attempts to control her and started fighting back. Then came the battles David hated so much.

However, Cindy would be a lot like Rachel; she wouldn't put up with any nonsense. The image of Rachel and Cindy sort of intermingled vaguely in his mind.

"Anyway, I don't mean to make a speech," her voice softened, "it's just that life is so short, I want to make as few mistakes as possible. And one way to avoid mistakes, as far as we—and marriage—are concerned, is to take our time. It's not like we live halfway around the world from each other, after all," she kidded. "We can still see each other later on, when we want to."

David looked rather crestfallen.

"I do care for you," she emphasized, "very much. And I think we could have a good—a great—marriage, and come back here for every anniversary if we wanted!" She grinned with David as they glanced about.

"But I just want to be sure. As I've said before, we've only known each other for a short time—maybe twelve or thirteen days—" they both grinned, "and have spent every day together… which has been a good thing." Both fell back to memories of the time spent. "But that's small compared to what's needed," she added.

"It takes time to get to know everything about another person, especially someone you might marry—time that's needed to change 'love' into that serious meaning we talked about." Cindy took a deep breath and gently continued, "That's why we shouldn't make any promises to each other which might prove hard to keep." She paused, watching David's face.

"We should date other people, do things with them, see what's out there to compare each other to. Then we'll be satisfied that we've each done the best that we can, if we still think we're the ones for each other. I don't want any regrets, and you don't, either. There are enough regrets that come later in life anyway, so let's avoid that one."

They both fell silent and let their eyes wander from each other to the sea, the sky, and back again. It was said; it was decided. They both knew that this was the best—indeed, the only— choice open to them. It tore at their hearts to face the separation, yet within each of them, they sensed that it was right.

It was a bittersweet understanding of the present, but the hope of a future lay stretched before them, reaching into the far distant horizon, but nevertheless within their grasp. It was enough. It would do for now.

"I'd better get back," Cindy finally broke the spell.

"I guess so," David replied, slowly. "Thanks for the help," he joked, and they both smiled at the double meaning of boat scrubbing and deciding.

"No problem." Cindy kissed him, holding his head gently in her hands.

They got up, stretched their aching muscles, unaccustomed to the strain of the scrubbing action on the boat's hull, and limped back to board the dinghy. As they rounded the headland separating the two coves, both boats came into full view.

A sharp pang of conflicting desires now tore at them, one to stay on *Endeavor* and give in to their welling emotions, and another to go on to *Dawn Treader*, and let the planned course of events take place.

Cindy's mother waved, as she stepped from the ketch's cockpit and saw the approaching dinghy, and they both waved back. David eased the oars back into the clear water and leaned into the stroke.

29

Dennis and Colleen were pleased to have David sail along with them as far as Puerto Rico, since they indeed had parental concerns about someone as young as David out sailing by himself, and they openly said so—also giving him some jerry jugs of fuel, since he was nearly out.

David was inwardly warmed by the concern they showed, and didn't resent it at all. Moreover, them saying that he was like a part of the family to them, now that they had spent so much time together, also made him happy, since he figured it was one more step he had made toward the eventual goal of gaining Cindy's hand in marriage.

Together, the family laid out the charts and discussed tactics for sailing the remaining distance to San Juan. Dennis had some good pointers about how they could handle the trade wind, since it would be from their general direction of travel, and David listened intently.

After a light dinner, David excused himself to get back to his boat, to put things in order for their early departure the next day. They too had quite a bit of straightening up to do to get ready, and were already beginning the task when David pulled away in his dinghy.

Early that morning, David pulled anchor and motored over to the ketch. After a few brief comments about the direction of the wind—from the northeast and not too bad—both boats headed out the south channel, through the reef.

As the wind filled the sails, and *Endeavor* began to creak and groan her familiar chorus, David looked back to the small island, already beginning to diminish in size.

Undoubtedly, he'd had some of the happiest days of his life there, and felt as though a part of him was being cast away. But, as he turned and looked at the sea ahead, brilliant deep blue and lightly frosted with small whitecaps, he reconciled his remorse with the fact that at least he had some memories which would last a lifetime—and a possible future to last just as long with the girl he loved. This hope made the parting more tenable, and he set about trimming the sails.

Although the larger ketch could sail faster than the little sloop, Dennis kept the distance between the two boats fairly constant. Sometimes they would be almost within shouting distance of each other, and Cindy would sit on the aft deck, braced against the heel of the boat, and watch David. They would wave occasionally and try to mime messages to each other, in a game which went on and on, with only a few successes at interpreting the content. But it didn't matter; it was fun and made the time pass quickly.

During the night, it was more difficult to keep track of each other, or even the running lights they both kept on. It was especially hard when they tacked off in different directions to the wind, which persisted in coming from the direction they wanted to go.

As David became sleepier, he knew he would have to forget about keeping track of them and get some sleep. He'd try to locate them again in daylight.

Keeping a careful plot of his track with GPS positions, he set up a system of sleeping with the autopilot on for an hour, and then keeping watch for three or four hours, whichever he could stand. And so it went, through the night.

At daybreak, David scanned the horizon to locate the ketch, but saw not a sign of it. Disheartened, and with a few strings of fear tugging at his confidence, he stared hard at the chart. According to his calculations they should have been nearby, but climbing up from below and looking out into the gray morning sea, he was reminded of how vast that ever-moving body of water was and knew they could indeed be quite close and him not see them. Yet, however well he was aware of that fact, the memory stung. He tried the handheld VHF radio Dennis had loaned him, but they were too far away.

Well, nothing to do but go on. Keep on the planned course and wait for either their boat or San Juan to show up first. That made him feel better, and he made up a super breakfast from ingredients he had borrowed.

Late in the afternoon, the wind veered more to the north—a welcome change, since it meant that he would be able to sail on longer tacks more directly toward his landfall. Just before dusk, he thought he spotted *Dawn Treader's* sails in the far distance, ahead of him and to the south, but he wasn't sure. An attempt at contact with the VHF didn't help.

The temptation to change course and go toward the sighting was very strong, but he now knew better; it might not have been them, or might even have been a cloud. Besides, who was to say that perhaps they weren't the ones who were off-course and not him? *Best to stay with my own calculations.* At least he knew where he was—better than running off somewhere unknown.

The second night passed like the first. There was no moon, so the only light he had was that of the stars, and they cast an ethereal light with no competition from man-made sources. David found that they even provided a sort of companionship as he sat out in the darkness of the sea, protected by the cockpit from the hissing and gurgling water, which stretched unbroken for hundreds… thousands of miles all about him, and for thousands of feet beneath.

He watched the stars progress across the sky, and noticed some new ones just barely visible on the southern horizon. He wondered what lay just beneath them, on the surface of the Earth. For the first time in his life, David was increasingly curious about what lay beyond the unseen, beyond the frontiers of his rather protected youthful experience.

He had never shared his father's eagerness to explore, his curiosity about the half-hidden mechanisms of the natural world. In contrast, David was always too absorbed in surviving the social one into which he was cast.

But now he felt freer, more stable than ever before. And he knew it had something to do with a female human being, somewhere out there in the obscurity of the night and immense ocean.

His last thoughts, before falling asleep for the last time that night, were of wondering if she, too, was thinking similarly of him, and the huge gulf which now separated them.

When he awoke, the sun was already fairly high, and beginning to warm the sea air. He quickly stumbled topside to glance about. He had overslept, having shut off his alarm and gone back to sleep. The autopilot steadily moved the steering wheel back and forth, in counter-rhythm to the marching swells. He was thankful for that, and reprimanded himself to be more vigilant next time.

It was mid-morning when he joyfully spotted two sails directly ahead. To add to his delight, a dark-blue bulk of land was slowly emerging from the tall, stationary cloud mass which formed over the high mountains of Puerto Rico.

I'm right on course!

All morning the two boats sailed close together, with the steep, forested mountains of the island looming in the near distance. They first sighted the headland of Punta Puerto Nuevo, only twenty miles from San Juan, and made good time despite the contrary trades. By afternoon, they were sailing into San Juan.

30

David had dreamed many times, during the first few days after the accident, of being able to sail into a port such as this. He had envisioned himself coming in, to the surprise of unsuspecting yachtsmen, weather-beaten and haggard, but heroically mustering up the strength to set his father's rescue into motion.

But those dreams had long since crumbled with the ravages of reality, to be replaced by the necessity of survival and then a hopeful future. Now the two boats silently sailed steadily closer to the end of his trials and uncertainty—and the reality of unfamiliar civilization.

David had lived in large cities all his life, and thought he was accustomed to the contrast they provided to rural areas, but he hadn't counted on the degree to which he had been conditioned by the isolation of the past month.

Thankfully, Dennis took the lead in *Dawn Treader*, as the boats entered the channel into the busy harbor. David was all eyes and wonder, as they began to meet large ships and small workboats, noisily jockeying for position in the narrow channels, and at the numerous wharves.

But the thing which struck David foremost was the imposing fortress of El Morro, standing boldly on the tip of the long, flat peninsula of Old San Juan, which formed the protective bulwark against the ceaseless Atlantic waves. In the afternoon sun, the fortress did not look as menacing as it would in the early morning, but instead seemed warm and inviting as it basked in the sunlight, which played upon the mottled tan and gray stone walls and battlements.

The sense of protection and security David felt, as he sailed close under the fort and its supporting cliffs, somehow seemed extremely appropriate to him. He heard a voice calling, and he glanced forward to see Cindy waving to him and pointing vigorously at the ancient citadel. She too was affected by the view and the moment. He waved back, and then turned his attention to the looming buildings ahead.

At first it was difficult for David to figure out exactly where Dennis was going, since they seemed to be headed directly into a maze of shipping facilities and buildings. But, in a short while, he was able to distinguish the office buildings and high-rise hotels beyond a busy bridge, and see that yacht marinas were coming up.

To David, though, even the boats at the slips, as well as those anchored in San Antonio Channel, were swallowed up by the immensity of the man-made environment, and the activity which bustled about them. He told himself that it wasn't such a big place in comparison to many back in the States, but it was still very unsettling. He felt very much out of place, and his thoughts kept drifting back to the peaceful islands he had just left a few days ago, now seemingly years in the past.

After tying up at the transient float in a marina, Dennis and David were able to get cleared with Customs and Immigration before the office closed. Since *Dawn Treader* had stayed longer at Esperanza Island than planned, Dennis was insistent on immediately continuing toward the Virgins the next day, while David would stay to contact his parents. Getting customs out of the way would allow them to make an early departure but, more than that, it meant that David and the family could go ashore that evening and do some sightseeing.

Once the boats were anchored off to the side of the channel, the five of them put on their best shore clothes and headed back to land. They forsook the bright lights of the beach hotels and restaurants past the bridge, and instead went into Old San Juan, where they wandered the narrow streets and found various excuses for sampling new edible treats, and looking at the latest offerings in curios and art.

Everyone thoroughly enjoyed themselves, at times becoming self-conscious of their rather raucous public behavior, but not regretting sharing the joy of a much-needed landfall. Yet none of the locals seemed to mind, but instead simply joined in the laughter and contributed to the celebration of the occasion. It was late at night when everyone was finally exhausted, and fell into the dinghy for the short ride to their anchorage.

The noise of the harbor and city awakened David rudely the next morning; he still wasn't accustomed to all the activity. He groaned lightly in pain, from the muscles which ached after being used rather intensively for sailing in the last two days; he had gotten lazy from the more measured activity at the island.

But he also groaned because it meant that Cindy was leaving him. The thought was intolerable, and he wrestled with it momentarily, but soon decided it was too hot to stay below. The air was heavy and stifling, and he struggled to the cockpit.

"Hey, sleepyhead!" a voice called across the water. He turned toward *Dawn Treader* and saw Cindy, waving to him and laughing. He waved her away, sat heavily on the cockpit bench, and held his head between his hands. He just couldn't get going.

Soon, though, he became aware of more activity aboard the ketch and looked up. All the family was busy with their assigned "ready to leave" chores. In a little while, Cindy got into their dinghy and headed over toward him.

"Good morning, Sunshine!" She was oppressively cheerful. She tied off the dinghy and hoisted herself aboard.

David grunted a greeting and leaned back against the cabin bulkhead. "How come you're so cheerful?" he groaned. "I'd think you'd be sad about leaving."

"I am… very sad. But that doesn't mean I have to act that way… like some people I know," she chided. "It doesn't help to mope; that won't make me feel any better. So, I'm cheerful!"

The logic of her reasoning mostly escaped David, but her smile and radiance didn't. He grinned. "You're crazy, you know that? Crazy."

"Yup, I'm crazy," she cheerfully agreed. And then added, slightly more somberly, "Crazy about you."

"I'm crazy about you, too."

Their eyes met for a moment, then Cindy broke off and swung down the companionway. "Good grief!" the exclamation drifted up. "What a mess!" Her head popped up. "Don't you ever clean up?"

"Hey, it's not that bad," he countered.

"Well, it certainly could use a woman's touch," Cindy argued, as she climbed back up. They both grinned at each other. It was great to feel so much at ease together.

"Well, I've got to get back and help out."

"I know," David regretfully agreed. "But I don't want you to go."

"I don't want to, either, but it's got to be." And then, regaining her cheerful composure, "It's not—"

"—like we're on opposite sides of the world," David finished. The little joke made it easier and, with the words said, more relaxed about the tension of the parting.

"I've got to go," Cindy repeated, and reached toward David. They embraced in a light kiss, then held each other for a moment before letting go. "See you soon."

"Soon," David replied, and Cindy climbed back over the side, into the dinghy.

As *Dawn Treader* pulled away an hour later, David waved

goodbye to the other members of the family, their real goodbye having been said last night.

Cindy walked to the stern of the ketch as it passed David. Grasping the stern railing, she lifted one hand in a brief wave. Her lips formed the words that David waited for, and he repeated them.

In a short time, her figure was indistinguishable from the boat, and David went below.

Endeavor's cabin now seemed extremely silent and very empty. And in a bit of a mess, David had to agree. He started picking up odds and ends of gear and clothing, but one thing was new: when he glanced at the chart table, a white envelope lay on it. He stepped over to get it. *"David"* was written on the outside, in Cindy's handwriting.

He felt a warm glow inside, as he climbed to the cockpit and looked hard in the direction of the ketch. He could just see it, as it turned out of the channel, its white sails filling gently like lifting wings. He smiled and lifted out the note inside.

"Dearest David,

"I just couldn't part without one last goodbye, even if it had to be in this form. Despite my cheerful outward appearance, I'm very much torn up about having to part. It's just the way I handle things. Maybe I'd be better off just showing how I feel, like you do, rather than trying to disguise it. But that's the way I am.

"I care a lot for you, David, and love you very much, in our special way. So much that it hurts me to think of the time we must spend apart. And yet I know it is for the best, like we discussed, and I know you feel the same way.

"Now you have to face your task by yourself. I would like to be there to help and comfort you, but I can't, and I think this might be best anyway. After all, it's something that you have to meet and come to terms with. I just want you to know that I have confidence in your ability to withstand whatever trauma might be waiting, and that you

will be able to make good judgments in the face of it. Just remember, I'm there with you in spirit, if not in person. Have faith in yourself— and me.

"*With you always,*

"*Love Cindy.*"

David choked up and tears formed, but he didn't fight them. They were tears of compassion and love, better reasons for such cannot be found.

PART THREE

31

It took David the rest of the morning to muster enough courage to go to a telephone ashore, but he finally set off to find one. In a few moments he found several phone kiosks, but they were open to the street, and he couldn't imagine competing with that noise while he was trying to give his message.

He went back to the marina office and explained that he needed more privacy. The secretary at the office thought for a moment, then suggested he go to a telecommunications office a short distance away. She warned him that it was old and not so nice—a hold-over from an earlier level of technology—but that it did offer inside privacy. David thanked her and started walking.

The office was in an ancient stone building, which had a new façade put on perhaps fifty years ago. The result was that neither the smooth marble of the facing, nor the dirty tan of the rough-hewn old stone on the sides, gave the building any dominant character; it still looked like an unfinished inspiration of nationalism. Inside the busy entrance corridor, he found a directory—it was in Spanish, but the word for "telephone" still looked pretty much the same.

Locating the office, he was confronted by a room with two glassed-in clerks sitting behind a long, tall counter. On the opposite side was a row of ten doors, which opened into tiny phone booths. A loudspeaker would frequently call a name and number, and someone would get up from the row of nearby seats and slide into one of the booths.

The morning was well-progressed by now, and the heat of the

day was accumulating in the stuffy old building. It was very hot, almost suffocating, since no breeze could reach down the narrow, confined streets and through the ineffective open windows. David wondered how people could stand to be in those enclosed boxes for very long, but he guessed he'd soon find out.

He stood in line, in front of the glassed counter, and soon reached a clerk. She wasn't too enthused about helping David, but he noticed the same robot-like response with other customers, so he wasn't offended. He gave the necessary information for phoning collect, and turned to take a seat. There wasn't one available at first, but soon he was able to grab one, when a large woman took her three kids with her to a phone booth. The humid air seemed to hang about him like an invisible weight and he perspired freely, adding his sweat to the odor of those around him.

The wait seemed endless, and he began to worry about being able to decipher his name and number when it was called. The announcements by the clerks all seemed to sound the same, regardless of what was said.

With all the confusion and his worrying, he was very distracted and had to remind himself several times what he was there for, going over in his mind what he would say. He retraced the most recent days, and that was as far as he could ever get. His mind couldn't stay focused long enough to formulate anything. Besides, the heat was beginning to make him extremely uncomfortable.

David began to feel slightly faint and nauseated, and thought he might have to leave the room, when the man sitting next to him nudged him back into awareness, and told him in English that they were calling him on the loudspeaker: number six. Half aware of what he was doing, David murmured "Thanks" to the man, walked to the booth which had been pointed out, and peered past the slightly opened door.

He pulled it open the rest of the way, stepped in, and closed it. In the dimmed light he could make out the single receiver on a phone hook. The small booth smelled of the sweat of the many occupants earlier that day. He stared at the black handset, then reached up and took it down.

"Hello?" he said rather warily, not certain that this wasn't a dream.

"Hello... David?" a woman's voice answered, equally uncertain. "David, is that you?"

"Rachel? It's me. I'm calling from San Juan."

"From where?"

"San Juan, Puerto Rico." He waited for some acknowledgment, since there was a lot of static, then continued. "Let me talk..." he choked for a moment, "let me talk to Dad." There, he'd said it; it was out. He waited expectantly.

There was no immediate answer.

"David, are you okay? Are you alright? I didn't know—"

"Let me talk to Dad, Rachel," he interrupted. "I need to talk to Dad." There was a pleading in his voice, as he struggled to close the last link in the circle of events. This wasn't what he had expected. Something was wrong.

"David," her voice was louder and more firm, "there's something we've got to talk about."

No! I want Dad. He didn't want to hear, and the demons of repressed doubt began to pour out of their caves. "I want to talk to Dad," he emphasized each word.

"David, listen to me! I want you to listen to what I have to say."

He didn't want to. He sensed what she was going to say, and he didn't want to hear it. From the start of this horrible ordeal, fears and recriminations dominated his mind, but with the visit by the fishermen, hope and belief in salvation took over and quickly grew into a welcome assumed reality.

But now, he began to perceive the tumbling events of the past early weeks, as they likely truly were. He felt as though he were swelling up and going to burst. The gray walls of the booth hovered over him, pressing tighter and tighter.

"David, are you still there? Answer me, please, David." Rachel's voice no longer sounded strong and guiding; it was the voice of sorrow and loneliness. "David?" she softly asked again, and waited.

Finally, the walls were no longer closing in on him. They were just musty plywood sheets, wearily laden with the graffiti of countless poor memories for numbers. "I'm here," came his distant voice.

"David, your father is dead," she almost choked on the word, but managed it. "He was found over three weeks ago by another sailboat. The body wasn't in good shape, but it was identified as him."

David couldn't reply. His mind was bouncing in and out, through past hopes and reality. He was just worn out, numb from his past recriminations and guilt. So, he just listened—and opened his mind to accept the truth.

"He had tied survival gear to himself, but…" her voice stopped and then started again, "he was just out there too long, without any water, in the sun."

The receiver went dead again and then came to life. "The funeral was two weeks ago. I held off, hoping you'd make it back in time," David could hear her crying, and then struggle to control it, "but you never came. I didn't know where you were, or what happened. I need to know… we need to talk."

David was frozen. In that hot steam box, he was unable to do anything, talk, cry, scream, swear… nothing. He couldn't move. All the worst of his horrible imaginings, from way back when he first discovered that his dad was gone, were true. His dad had been calling to him, screaming at the dark shadow of a boat which swiftly left him behind. Screaming for his son to wake up and help him, to rescue him.

But David had slept on, comfortably in bed, irritated at having to wake up when the boat lurched, because the sails were out of trim. And his dad, the man who made him, was slowly rotting away in the sun and water, waiting for his son to return, weakly calling out his name—until he could call no more.

It was anger that had finally moved David to do anything that horrible night and the following days, and brought him to curse everything and himself in fits of passion. It was a pointless thing to do, and he sensed it even then, as his mind raged.

So there was no point in letting that anger resurface now. He had been through all the accusations and recriminations and remorse a zillion times before. And it got him nowhere.

Face it, the worst happened. The fishermen were wrong and so was my wanting to believe… Now I have to go on.

Rachel waited for as long as she could, to give him the privacy she detected he needed just now, then she tentatively broke in, "David, are you alright, honey?"

Finally, he answered, "I'm here." His voice cracked and tried to gather strength, as it trembled. "I'm okay, really I am." And he started to cry, despite his best efforts. "It's just that I had hoped, so much… that it wouldn't be this way. I started to believe it…" It took a moment for him to gain some control. "This just took me by surprise," he managed to squeak out. There was a brief pause on the other end.

"Listen, I'm going to catch the first flight I can get on—today, if possible—and I'll be down there with you."

David began to protest at first, but Rachel cut him off. "I know you think it's not necessary—maybe that you don't even want me to—but I'm coming. I…" she emphasized, "need to be with you. I think we need each other." And she added, "So, I'm coming."

Not a sound on David's end.

"Where can I find you?"

"We're anchored out in the harbor, off the San Juan Bay

Marina, where all the yachts are," he finally replied. "It'll be easy to locate us."

"Us?"

"Yeah, the boat and me."

A pause, then, "I'll be there as soon as I can. You'll be okay?" She was always such a worrier about him.

"Of course. I'll be fine."

"Alright. I'll… see you when I get there."

"Yep." David paused. "Rachel… I'm glad you're coming." He couldn't help it. The welling sense of relief, and need for a certain closeness just now, was too much for him to deny.

The sound of a throat being cleared rasped over the phone. "I'm glad, too, David. Goodbye."

"Bye."

And the phone went dead.

He held the humming receiver for a few seconds, not quite willing to let go, then clacked it into its cradle. Opening the door, the noise and people in the office startled him—like opening a door into another world. So absorbed had his attention been on the phone call that he stared bewildered, and then stumbled out of the building.

He gulped the fresh air and leaned wearily against the warm stone. *Now what?*

He felt rather groggy—from the jarring of a long-distance call, the news, the unfamiliar city bustle, the different culture— and stood watching the traffic of cars and people pass by.

Slowly, his mind began to organize. *Rachel couldn't make it here until…* He glanced at his watch. It wasn't there. Then he remembered he had forgotten to put it on. No clocks in sight, either. He finally asked a passer-by and calculated. She couldn't get here until tonight at the earliest, and probably not until tomorrow.

He then began to aimlessly wander, flowing with the crowd from plaza to plaza, past old cathedrals, new and old shopping areas, and eventually found himself walking along the jutting peninsula which served as the foundation for El Morro—the castle which used to protect the harbor, during early years of colonial island-grabbing, and days of piracy.

David stood out on the farthest rampart and watched the ocean swells leap at the walls of the old fort. Wave after wave endlessly broke and gathered again, and seagulls wheeled on the air currents. The moist trade wind blew steadily, and he leaned slightly into it.

Now that he was alone and not distracted, he was more aware of how unusual it was to not have the continual boat motion, so used to it as he was, and he stood there for some time enjoying the unfamiliar feeling of solid footing.

Without any awareness of purpose, David ambled off and started to explore the fort, walking from one promontory to another, following this walkway, that passageway, and emerging on another level. He was thinking about the lives of the men who defended this city, and of the lives of the men, women, and children of the city's past. How strange it seemed. They lived their lives and died, and hardly a trace of their once important— at least, to them—thoughts, emotions, and deeds remained.

He glanced at the pounding waves, the singular clouds passing by, which quickly coalesced into the large mass hanging over the island, and watched the tourists and local people. Several families were out wandering over the ruins, absorbed in their immediate enjoyment and togetherness.

He seemed out of place somehow, being alone as he was. Yet, at the same time, it was a sense of peace that he felt, an understanding that this is simply the way life is—the timelessness, the endlessly repeating patterns, some joyful and some painful. The way it will always be, regardless of how he or anyone else might wish it. Loneliness also comes and goes. Companionship does as well, but there is always the possibility of a new and lasting one; another part of life's repeating patterns.

It was getting mid-afternoon and he was hungry. There were some interesting-looking snack shops he had passed somewhere earlier. *I'll try one of them.*

Besides, the thought resurfaced, *Rachel might yet make it in tonight.*

32

And so she did. It was early evening and David was down below, straightening up the boat without much enthusiasm. He had already grown weary of checking every small boat's motor sound which seemed to be heading his way, and so didn't bother with any more of them. But this one was persistent, and he glanced out of the companionway.

A dark-haired woman waved and, as David peered more closely, he could make out her face. It was Rachel.

The water-taxi driver deftly pulled the small skiff alongside, and hung on while Rachel paid him his fee, handed David a small duffel bag, and swung on board. The elderly man then pushed off and left the two confronting each other.

Neither said a word for a moment, then slowly reached out to each other in an embrace. In the past, David never let her give him any kind of hug, especially not since he had gotten bigger, but this time it seemed natural. *She looks like she could use it,* he thought to himself, and lied about his own feelings. But the closeness of the contact felt good to him, and served to break some of the tension and unfamiliarity which remained.

"So," Rachel said in a relieved voice, and looked him up and down with that adult "my-how-you've-grown" scrutiny. "You certainly look healthy." She managed a broad smile and, to draw a little warmth out of David, added. "You haven't been starving."

"Nope," he managed, without too much difficulty. It was hard without his dad there as the connecting link. In the past, even when he wasn't physically present, his dad provided the reason why this boy and this woman had strings of attachment. Now that reason was gone, and both felt the vacuum. "Have a nice flight?" He couldn't think of anything else.

"Oh, yes, I did. I was lucky and got a cancellation. I only had time to throw a few things in a bag before I had to run to the airport."

David glanced down at the small, soft-sided duffel as though it were hiding a bomb.

"I figured I could always buy a few clothes if I needed them, depending on how long…" She stopped. "Let's sit down, huh?"

"Sure. Uh, want some lemonade or something?" He moved to go below, to stir some up.

"Yes, I'd love some! It's so beastly hot." She laughed lightly and undid a paisley scarf she had knotted at her throat. She lifted the large, floppy collar of her loose maroon blouse and flapped it with both hands, several times, to get some air flowing. The peasant-style skirt she wore hung down in loose folds, revealing bare feet with strap marks still showing, from the sandals she had just kicked off.

Rachel had a lovely olive complexion, which was set off by her black hair. Her features were all rather delicate, in contrast to David's birth mother, and she looked fragile, but that wasn't the case at all. She had a quick smile—too quick, David sometimes thought—which gave her face a pleasant attractiveness.

She was also rather energetic and not content to sit alone; she immediately clambered down the ladder behind David.

Rachel stood and silently looked around, then sat down on the settee. David resented her presence down below, but wasn't quite sure why.

"You've kept things up well, David."

The clink of stirring liquid in a glass continued.

"We've all had many memories—good memories—in this boat. Actually, I sometimes think I married this boat, too; your father used to spend so many hours working on it, and loved it so much."

The clinking became more boisterous and stopped. "Here," David thrust the glass at her. His face was dark with rising anger. He sat on the settee and, in a few gulps, downed the contents of his. He clanked the empty glass on the dinette table and stared off into space. Something was happening, but he couldn't nail it down. This wasn't how he wanted it at all. Frustration swelled his chest and he had trouble breathing.

Rachel sipped her lemonade and watched him. "David," she softly broke the silence, "it isn't any good like this. It doesn't solve anything. We have to talk about what happened—about us and the future; what we're going to do."

She paused to set her shoulders, ready for what was to come.

"And first," Rachel leaned in toward David and gently took his hands, "I need to know what happened. Not because I'm angry or want to hurt you in any way—and I know it's very, very hard for you to talk about it—but we both need to get it out and exposed… shared… so it's something we both have in common and can put in the past."

David eyed her closely and, watching the determined but gentle confidence she conveyed, he felt a little bit safer. He resisted at first.

But, as the tale unwound, he more freely related the discovery of his dad's disappearance: his feelings of responsibility for not waking up, of incompetence at handling the boat, his indecisions about what to do, and fears of the consequences of his actions. He had once again launched into the blackness of that night, only this time he had a fellow companion on that treacherous road of emotions.

He also related his discoveries regarding his dad's wisdom and advice about the boat, and making needed decisions—as well as remorse about his behavior, as such a stubborn son.

Rachel listened intently as the story unfolded, but it became an intenseness of love for a teenager trying to put wrongs to right, as best he could—not an intenseness of resentment.

When it came to the fishermen and their misinformation, with tears welling, she could relate to David's feelings of being willfully misled by his eagerness to believe the best outcome of the encounter, such as an inexperienced teenager would do in his situation. She knew that her news in the phone booth was truly devastating to David, and she fully understood the effect it had on him—bringing up once again her own feelings of panic, when she had received the same news by phone that terrible day, now gone by, but still smoldering deep within her emotional memory.

As the waves of passing boats gently rocked *Endeavor*, neither of them spoke for a few moments, so emotionally drained they were by the shared experience of the retelling and revealing that the story provided for each of them.

Rachael finally broke the silence. "Thank you so much, David. I know it was extremely difficult for you to do, but it was needed to clear the air, so we can both move on to the present… and the future… about us."

She waited, but David said nothing.

"We have to talk, David. We have to settle this thing between us," she encouraged.

David was trying to do as she asked—as he knew he must—but it was difficult. He turned to her, the rims of his eyes glistening. "I'm trying, Rachel. I really am. It's just that… well, let's be honest," he fought down the growing tightness in his throat, "I've never liked you, coming in and taking my mother's place, taking my dad away, and trying to tell me what to do. I hated you for it."

There! It was out at last, and David's dam of resentment began to crumble. He could see his words hurt Rachel, but, *Damn it all, she's the intruder. She's the one who insisted on coming down here. It's time this was all said.*

"I've just never been able to accept that. I know it's not fair— I can see that now—but that's the way it's been with me. I couldn't help it." He turned his head away from her and stared at his empty glass, feeling relieved at the release, but also pained at the effect his words must have on her.

The words did hurt, and her voice quavered in response, but she could also see beyond them. "I've known that, David, for years. Ever since you and I first met, the hate in your eyes read like a billboard advertisement. But I loved your father, very much, and I hoped you would eventually get over the resentment and come to love me, too, as I have loved you, as my son." She took a moment to settle a bit.

"You're the only one I've got, you know—probably the only son I'll ever have. That makes you very special to me. And, now that Gregory is gone... you're the only part of him I have left." The words choked her voice, but she managed to get them out.

It's true, David realized, the newness of the thought startling him. *I never thought of that before.* Now, he was the only link between the past—the only living link. She had her memories, of course, but as far as a living, breathing person goes... *I'm it. Unique. A special person to her.* He could see that. *But, what is she to me?*

"I value that very much," she continued, "and would like it if you did, too. I realize you've got your mother—though you don't see her too much anymore—and your memories. Besides, you're young and have a life yet to make for yourself. For you, there's a lot of time left for the pain of this tragedy to fade. There isn't for me," she stated, bluntly.

"I went through a lot of struggles to find a man like your father. I had my life set up, and was just beginning to enjoy the harvest of all the emotional turmoil and effort I had put into building the relationship... and then he was torn away from me. Just like that!" The sharp snap of her fingers forced David to look at her.

Her face was flushed slightly and a certain hardness—no, determination—tensed the muscles of her neck so that it stretched tightly, giving her an aura of hidden, cat-like strength.

He had seen this look before, when she and his father were hotly debating an issue. But the most startling realization was that Cindy had exactly the same expression when she was aroused.

"So, this is no flash in the pan for me, David. This was my best shot—probably my only one. And I'm determined to hold onto whatever I can of the man I love. I've been your mother for seven years now. Regardless of what you think, I've been your mother, loving you, looking after your needs, and caring about what happens to you. I'm the one who's done the daily dirty work, not Ellen. She comes and gets you for a weekend fun-fling, then drops you back with us. That's okay; I don't mind that too much, but when we get to talking about mothers, then I put my foot down, hard. That's where I want to count. Just because you're not from my womb, a part of my flesh and blood, doesn't mean that you are any the less my son... if you'll let it be."

Her eyes gripped David tightly, and he couldn't look away.

"Flesh has nothing to do with it. Your father and I had no flesh bond, but do you think that made our relationship any the less real, any the less valuable and enduring?"

Images of the island and talks with Cindy flashed in David's mind.

"Relationships are made, not born, David. I think your father's first marriage proved that," she added in a softer tone.

There was silence as Rachel caught her breath. Her face was a shade lighter, and as the tension receded she leaned back. "So, I'm a very stubborn and determined woman, and I don't easily let go of the people and things I love: your father, you, and even this old boat." She fondly stroked the polished wood. "There's a lot in this lady—some old, some new," she looked directly at him, "not all of it easy to see."

David stared at her. *She knows!* She knows about the boat, and what had happened between him and it: his father's presence; the boat; them being the same. But, how? How could she understand all that? *Well, maybe she doesn't know it all, but from watching Dad learn about the boat, she knows enough to be able to understand what I went through.*

And he suddenly realized that she was the only one who could truly ever completely understand and feel the relationship they shared, of husband and father and boat—the common bonds which linked them all forever.

David nodded slightly, cleared his throat, and tried to talk, to now turn the tide of his feelings for her, but the effort to tell her his part of the tragic story had overwhelmed him—and instead, he simply leaned forward and fell into her open arms… and cried. He sobbed with the release from his ill-placed past relationship with her, and the trauma of the tragedy with his dad. Rachel held him tightly to her body, as the terror of it all flowed out and was absorbed by her motherly comforting. Rachel softly cried in joy, as the final piece of being David's mom fell into place.

After a few minutes, David felt a lingering kiss on his forehead, as he began to regain control. They loosened their clasp but stayed close to each other, as they sat on the cabin settee. He felt he had shed the last part of the protective shell of his former self.

Telling Cindy about the tragedy had been a great help, but with Rachel, the final and necessary part of his new self had been fitted and sealed. The full sharing of both their pasts, and bringing them into a unified whole—the present—was uniquely theirs. And, as tragic as it was, this disaster forged a new link between them and the future.

33

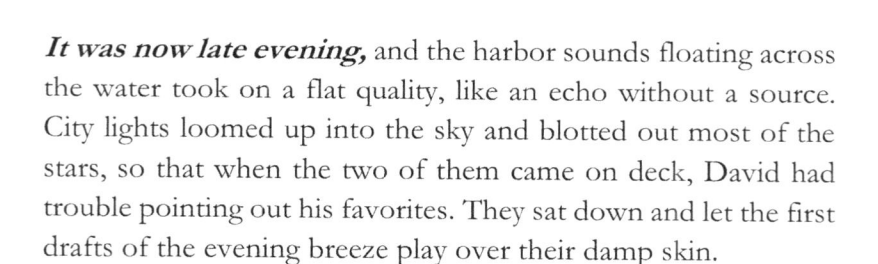

It was now late evening, and the harbor sounds floating across the water took on a flat quality, like an echo without a source. City lights loomed up into the sky and blotted out most of the stars, so that when the two of them came on deck, David had trouble pointing out his favorites. They sat down and let the first drafts of the evening breeze play over their damp skin.

"So, do you think you can stand your mother aboard for a few days?" Rachel suggested, her lips curling at the corners into an impish smile. Even though a great level of understanding and acceptance had been reached between them, the immediate future had not been discussed. "We can do things—whatever you'd like, here or someplace else. I think we just need to have some time together, before we get embroiled in life back home."

David looked long at her and grinned, "Sure. Of course." He paused. "Dad's cabin is clean; I moved out some gear today," he added, sheepishly. "I guess there's stuff we can do here…"

He thought hard for a minute, then looked very closely at his mother. A sly smile crept across his face. "How long do you have, anyway? I mean, could you stay maybe a week or two?"

Totally surprised, Rachel stammered, "I-I… well, I guess I could take that long, but I…" The intensely eager look on David's face froze her words. "I'd have to call into work and let them know I'm staying longer. Sure, I can do it," she beamed. "Why?"

"Well," he began, "I haven't told you everything. I didn't tell you about the drug smugglers—"

"Smugglers?!"

"—and there's also somebody I'd like you to meet." He paused to watch Rachel's expression. "Somebody pretty important to me. Her name's Cindy, and we're supposed to meet her and her parents in St. Thomas…"

The cabin lights of *Endeavor* glowed late that night, and the small sailboat rocked gently in the dark wakes of passing boats, murmuring satisfying gurgles of sound, from wavelets along its hull and breezes in its rigging—waiting patiently for journeys yet to come.

Glossary of Sailing Terms

Aft – toward the back end of a boat.

Autopilot – an instrument to automatically steer a boat.

Bow – the front of a boat.

Bimini – a cover over the cockpit.

Beat – to sail into the wind.

Beam – the width of a boat from the side.

Bulkhead – an inner wall structure across the beam.

Cabin – an inside area having a specific function, such as sleeping.

Chain locker – where anchor chain and line are stored.

Chronometer – a very accurate timekeeper; clock.

Companionway – entryway from the cockpit to inside the boat.

Cockpit – an area at the stern where steering is done, which has outside seating for crew.

Compass rose – the compass dial showing the four cardinal directions and 360-degree markings.

Dodger – a cover over the entrance to the companionway.

Dead-reckoning (D.R.) – navigation by estimating a boat's position on a map.

Fluky – variable, unsteady (winds).

Fore – toward the front end of a boat.

Forestay – a cable from the bow to the top of a mast.

Galley – the kitchen.

Halyard – a line using the mast to raise a sail.

Hanked – tied or shackled onto a line or stay.

Head – a small cabin with a toilet.

Heel – the tilting of a boat, over to the side opposite the wind.

Jib – a small, triangular sail hoisted on the forestay.

Knot – a boat's speed through water, equal to 1.15 mph.

Lee, leeward – opposite of the direction the wind is blowing from.

Luffing – (a sail) not completely filling with wind, and shaking the forward sail edge.

Lines – ropes named for specific uses on a boat.

Main, mainsail – the sail hoisted up a mast.

Nav station – an area inside the main cabin, where navigation equipment is located and used.

Mast – a tall pole for hoisting a sail.

Mast stay – a cable from the mast top to the deck, to support the mast.

Painter – a short line attached to the bow of a dinghy.

Parallel ruler – a pair of connected rulers, used for navigation with paper maps.

Port – while aboard, the left-hand side of a boat as you look toward the bow.

Reef – a reduction in sail area.

Rigging – the various lines and stays for supporting and operating a sailboat.

Round up – to head into the wind.

Rudder – a submerged appendage under the stern for steering.

Running before the wind – having the wind from behind.

Sloop – a sailboat with one mast.

Stern – the back end of a boat.

Stanchions – vertical poles supporting lifelines around the deck.

Stand watch – to be the person responsible for operating a boat during a specific time period of the day, especially at night.

Sextant – a navigation instrument which uses the position of the sun and other celestial objects to help determine location.

Stem to stern – from the front to the back of a boat.

Slatting – the violent flapping of a sail, when the wind is too weak to keep the sail full, or the sail is not properly trimmed.

Sheet – a line attached to the free end of a sail for control.

Spreader – a cross-structure on a mast helping to support the stays and mast.

Starboard – while aboard, the right-hand side of a boat as you look toward the bow.

Stay – typically a cable from the deck to the mast top, which supports the mast.

Tack – the direction the boat is going, relative to the wind.

Weigh anchor – to haul the anchor up and stow it aboard.

Winch – a spooling mechanism to take in and let out lines attached to sails, etc.

About the Author

Lance V. Packer was born on a farm in eastern Washington state. He grew up immersed in a close relationship with that world of structured nature, and had the time and freedom to think and wonder about what he observed around him, during the expansionist times of American life after World War II.

He was a youthful sponge, absorbing everything newly discovered—from ants underfoot, to distant glaciated volcanic peaks, to the attraction of the wiles of young girls with flashing eyes. All were approached enthusiastically, and sought for further exploration and questioning.

Years of further life adventures—including Peace Corps service, a Ph.D. in anthropology, twenty-seven years teaching public school in Alaska, and marriage to a wonderful woman—broadened that youthful experience. After a fourteen-year interlude, Lance has now returned to sailing adventures in the Caribbean.

Please share your thoughts and questions at the author's blog, forum, and website: https://www.lancepacker.com.

Also, posting your honest review at the book's sale page on Amazon.com can help spur other potential readers to consider the book.

Thank you.